Praise for Stuart McLean

"Stuart McLean is a natural storyteller with an ear cocked for real talk and a perfect sense of comic timing. In the modern line of Peter DeVries, Garrison Keillor, and fellow Canadian Stephen Leacock, McLean is a sly, entertaining humorist and an expert on the inexhaustible subject of human foibles."   —Billy Collins

"McLean draws his characters in such a way that we all know people just like them. . . . Terrific."   —*The Providence Journal*

"This folksy collection of stories follows a year in the life of Dave and Morley and their family. Christmas, summer camp, first dates, and other minutiae are covered in a warm and engaging manner. The stories . . . make for pleasant reading."   —*Booklist*

"An irresistible wit, warmth, and verve."
      —Ann-Marie MacDonald, author of *Fall on Your Knees*

"Think Garrison Keillor but with an urban twist. McLean is a natural storyteller, a modern Will Rogers if you will, with an ear for dialogue that is real and often laugh-out-loud funny."
                    —*The Tucson Citizen*

"Pure comic genius."   —*The Halifax Chronicle-Herald*

"Stuart McLean is a storyteller par excellence. . . . These are characters and situations that many readers will want to visit over and over."   —*Quill & Quire*

"Rip-roaringly funny . . . A cozy, meandering, often laugh-out-loud treat."   —*Kirkus Reviews*

"Warmhearted . . . funny . . . poignant . . . highly enjoyable."
                    —*Publishers Weekly*

STUART McLEAN

SECRETS FROM THE

VINYL CAFE

RIVERHEAD BOOKS
New York

RIVERHEAD BOOKS
Published by the Penguin Group
Penguin Group (USA) Inc.
375 Hudson Street, New York, New York 10014, USA
Penguin Group (Canada), 90 Eglinton Avenue East, Suite 700, Toronto, Ontario M4P 2Y3, Canada
(a division of Pearson Penguin Canada Inc.)
Penguin Books Ltd., 80 Strand, London WC2R 0RL, England
Penguin Group Ireland, 25 St. Stephen's Green, Dublin 2, Ireland (a division of Penguin Books Ltd.)
Penguin Group (Australia), 250 Camberwell Road, Camberwell, Victoria 3124, Australia
(a division of Pearson Australia Group Pty. Ltd.)
Penguin Books India Pvt. Ltd., 11 Community Centre, Panchsheel Park, New Delhi—110 017, India
Penguin Group (NZ), 67 Apollo Drive, Rosedale, North Shore 0632, New Zealand
(a division of Pearson New Zealand Ltd.)
Penguin Books (South Africa) (Pty.) Ltd., 24 Sturdee Avenue, Rosebank, Johannesburg 2196,
South Africa

Penguin Books Ltd., Registered Offices: 80 Strand, London WC2R 0RL, England

SECRETS FROM THE VINYL CAFE

This is a work of fiction. Names, characters, places, and incidents either are the product of the author's imagination or are used fictitiously, and any resemblance to actual persons, living or dead, business establishments, events, or locales is entirely coincidental. The publisher does not have any control over and does not assume any responsibility for author or third-party websites or their content.

Viking Canada hardcover edition / 2006
Viking Canada trade paperback edition / 2010
First Riverhead trade paperback edition: February 2011
Riverhead trade paperback ISBN: 978-1-59448-509-1

PRINTED IN THE UNITED STATES OF AMERICA

10   9   8   7   6   5   4   3   2   1

To Chris, Andrew and Robbie
with love

"Come, Watson, come!" he cried.
"The game is afoot."

SHERLOCK HOLMES

CONTENTS

PART 1

PASSION

OPERA

A lovely, long and romantic chapter, which begins in Cape Breton and ends at Yankee Stadium, wherein Dave's mother, Margaret, falls in love with music, a man and a mango—though the discerning reader will recognize the author's ruse, noting that he is simply using the story to declare his deep affection for New York City, and maybe even for his friend Robert K., whose absence in this story is notable.

Dave's mother, Margaret, had a difficult summer. She couldn't get warm. Everyone kept complaining about the heat and Margaret thought, *Are they nuts? It's freezing here.* At the beginning of July her daughter, Annie, drove up from Halifax. Annie found Margaret in her garden, wearing a sweater and a toque. Annie was wearing shorts and a T-shirt.

Margaret stared at her daughter and said, "Aren't you cold?"

On Sunday, as Annie was getting ready to leave, Margaret said, matter-of-factly, "Will you come up for my birthday? It's going to be my last."

"It was eighty-two degrees when I left," said Annie to Dave on the phone. "She was wearing a scarf. And gloves."

Dave and Annie and their families all went for Margaret's birthday. Dave and Morley gave her a garden diary, bound in leather.

"You can use it every year, to keep track," said Dave, flipping through the diary for her. "There's a place for everything. When things come up. The first frost."

"Don't be silly," huffed Margaret. "Just how many years do you think I've got left?"

It was Annie who bought her mother the tickets to the opera—to the Lincoln Center in New York City, to a Saturday afternoon at the Met.

Margaret said, "I can't possibly go to New York."

"Why not?" said Annie.

"I have nothing to wear," said Margaret, buttoning the top of her cardigan.

We stumble on the great loves of our lives in the oddest ways. Opera came to Margaret when she was a little girl. It arrived in the form of Doogie MacDougal—of the Ignish MacDougals, not the North Shore MacDougals.

Like his daddy, and his daddy before him, Doogie MacDougal was born and raised to the sea. He was a sailor four years on the *Margaree,* a rusty cargo ship that worked the eastern seaboard down to the Caribbean. Four years to sea, and he would have been gone forty more, except Doogie tore his shoulder to shreds in Boston unloading pallets of raw sugar. His arm twisted in a cargo net, yanking him fifteen feet in the air. He screamed like a seagull.

Doogie ended up in a New York hospital for a month and a half. A week before he was released, Angus MacDonnell showed up. He stood at the end of the bed, smoking, and said, "A man could get a job to the theatre if he wanted."

Doogie said, "I don't know squat about theatre."

Angus took a drag of his smoke and said, "Now tell me what's the difference between hauling ropes to change a scene and tying off a pallet. Rope's rope."

Doogie shrugged, and two months later he was drinking at McSorley's and working at the Met.

This was before unions. Before theatre schools. Half the backstage crew were crippled Bluenosers. Like Angus had said, rope's rope.

This was at the old Met, the one on Thirty-ninth and Broadway, before that building was torn down and the opera moved into the Lincoln Center. Back when Margaret was eleven years old. Back when Dr. Sandberg was the only person in Irish Bay who owned a radio. On Saturday afternoons, as many as fifty people would cram into his living room. Dr. Sandberg would turn his radio up and they would listen to their Doogie MacDougal at work. *Saturday Afternoon at the Met.* Milton Cross on the CBC.

That was in the early thirties, before the war.

Margaret, eleven years old, would go with her mother. They would dress up and sit on Dr. Sandberg's couch, leaning against each other, applauding with everyone else every time Milton Cross described a scene change. They could hear the audience in New York applauding too, and in her mind's eye Margaret could see Doogie MacDougal of Irish Bay, Cape Breton, standing on the stage of the Metropolitan Opera House in New York City, in front of the gold curtain, taking his bows. Doogie MacDougal gets caught up in rope and Margaret gets caught up in opera, and seventy-two years later there's probably no one in the country who has heard more of the Saturday afternoon broadcasts from the Met on the CBC than Margaret MacNeal from Irish Bay, Nova Scotia.

Sure enough, it was Doogie MacDougal who opened the door, but it wasn't Doogie who kept Margaret coming back. From the beginning she was swept away by the passion of the music. Opera is a world moved by storms and, living by the ocean, Margaret understood the eloquence of stormy weather. She was born into a world battered by elements beyond anyone's control. So she felt at home in this universe of villains and spurned lovers.

Opera was a world that made her feel worldly. By the time she was fourteen, Margaret had persuaded her father to buy a radio of their own, and every Saturday Margaret would sit in the parlor listening to her opera. You would think a parent could ask for nothing more, but Margaret's mother and father soon learned opera was leading their daughter astray.

The first time Margaret was moved to liquor, she was sixteen. Home alone, listening to *Tosca*, Margaret was overcome by the passions of Italy. The call of red wine stirred in her soul. There was no wine in the house, of course, or anywhere in town, except for the church. But that didn't stop Margaret. Margaret took one of her father's beers and mixed it with grape juice. She was passed out on the sofa when her parents came home. Sixteen and head over heels in love—drunk with love— all Margaret needed was a man.

As she got older, after she had found that man, she still pursued her first love. She listened every week, and she followed the lives of the stars—especially Maria Callas. Callas who lived on the edge. Callas who lived danger- ously. Callas who left her husband for that rat Aristotle Onassis.

Margaret devoured all the gossip-page news about them. How Callas met Onassis at the film festival in Venice. How he came to London and threw a party for her at the Dorchester Hotel. How he decorated the room with thousands of roses and invited Churchill and Gary Cooper and Douglas Fairbanks, Jr. Soon after the party, Callas sold her apartment in Milan and moved to Paris— moved so she could be on Onassis's route between London and Monte Carlo. It was pure love. And in the face of such love, Onassis dumped Callas for that Jackie

Kennedy. Callas died of a broken heart. Her ashes were sprinkled over the Mediterranean where Onassis sailed his yacht.

Callas didn't just sing opera, she lived one. Margaret longed to live as recklessly as Callas. When Margaret met Charlie, she loved him to death, and she decided the most reckless thing she could do was marry him. After they were married, Margaret tried to love her Charlie as recklessly as she could.

Charlie loved music too. Margaret taught him about opera. He taught her to sing. They sang together driving the car, and they sang together doing the dishes. Margaret loved Charlie so much that even if Enrico Caruso had flown to Big Narrows and rented the Starlight Room at the Breakwater Hotel, filled it with carnations and thrown a party for Margaret, inviting all the great Canadian personalities, like Stompin' Tom Connors and Foster Hewitt and Mister Dressup, Margaret wouldn't have given him an ear.

But now Charlie was gone, and Margaret felt just like Maria Callas—alone, a lonely old widow who couldn't get warm—except Margaret was living in a house in Big Narrows instead of an apartment in Paris.

Annie phoned her mother at the end of August and said, "I can't come to New York with you. The orchestra is going to Japan. They changed the dates."

Annie plays in Symphony Nova Scotia.

"Is there someone else you could ask?" asked Annie.

Margaret cast around town. Bernadette and Winnie both said they would be delighted to go to New York with Margaret. But they both said the same thing about the Met. "Do we have to go to the opera?" they asked.

Margaret phoned Annie in Halifax. "Couldn't the orchestra go to Japan another time?" she asked.

Annie said, "I'll get more tickets. We'll go to New York after Christmas."

Margaret said, "Christmas is a long time away. I don't know about after Christmas."

They both knew what she meant. She meant, I'll be dead after Christmas.

"Don't be silly," said Annie.

Margaret agreed to go in January. But she still had those birthday tickets sticking in the hall mirror, and they were making her crazy. Her kids were so wasteful. The way they used the telephone, calling all the time, as if long distance cost nothing. And now Annie was prepared to see these birthday tickets go unused. She couldn't let them go to waste. She phoned Gallagher's.

Arnie Gallagher is Big Narrows's one-man band. His store on Water Street serves the town as florist, funeral home, gift store and travel agency.

"When's your flight?" asked Annie when she called a day later.

"Monday," said Margaret. Margaret omitted telling her daughter that she was going alone, omitted mentioning that flying had seemed like such an indulgence that she had bought a round-trip bus ticket. The Narrows to Sydney, Sydney to Halifax, Halifax to Montreal, Montreal to New York: thirty-eight hours straight.

It was while the bus was pulling out of Schenectady that Margaret began talking to Charlie. They had always planned to go to New York. It was going to be their big trip, their opera hajj ... their pilgrimage. They were going to visit all the stations of the cross. Then Charlie died, and here she was, going alone.

For years Margaret had written down their plans in a pink Hilroy notebook. Unfortunately, all her plans were gleaned from *The New Yorker* magazine. For years Margaret had had the only subscription in Cape Breton. Unhappily, she cancelled it in fury in 1987, when William Shawn was forced to step down as editor. All her New York information was at best fifteen years out-of-date.

She arrived at the Port Authority bus terminal in New York City at seven-thirty in the morning. Margaret, who had barely closed her eyes for two nights, had finally fallen into a deep sleep not an hour before. When the driver shook her awake, she had no idea where she was. She humped her suitcase onto Forty-second Street in a daze. She was hungry and overwhelmingly tired. She stared at the river of yellow taxi cabs, at the early-morning crush of the city. Instead of the rush of excitement she had been expecting, Margaret felt fear. The buildings were so tall and packed together that she could barely see the sky. Suddenly New York didn't seem like such a good idea.

"Charlie?" she said, looking all around, her hand at her throat.

A man on Rollerblades was heading down the sidewalk, towards Margaret. He had spiked hair and tattoos, and pins everywhere. There were pins in his nose and in his ears and in his lips and through his cheek. This "pin man," who was—oh my God, he was wearing a skirt—this "pin man" cut by Margaret on his Rollerblades, and she felt the flap of his skirt on her legs. She thought to herself that no one had mentioned anything in *The New Yorker* about pin men in skirts who brushed by you on their Rollerblades when you were standing on the sidewalk minding your own business.

And they hadn't mentioned the noise either. She had never read about the honking horns. Margaret backed up and leaned against the bus terminal. She felt dizzy. The wall felt grimy. Dirty. For five minutes she leaned against it. Then a man carrying a black briefcase walked by her, stopped, turned and handed her a dollar bill. She was too stunned to give it back. Her legs were shaking.

She went back into the bus station and sat on a bench. She and Charlie had planned to stay at the Algonquin Hotel. When she had phoned for a reservation, Margaret couldn't believe what they wanted for a room. She went to number two on their list: the Chelsea.

Somehow Margaret got herself going. Somehow she found the subway. It was terrifying. It reminded her of Margaret-Anne Madigan's vacuum cleaner—loud and dark and dirty. She got on the wrong train. It was heading north, which was not the way she should have been going, but she was too frightened to get off. Like the man in the song, she rode around and around for an hour and a half.

It was noon before she finally asked for help. She found herself standing on the corner of 125th and Adam Clayton Powell Jr. Boulevard, in the heart of Harlem, right across from the Apollo Theater, where Billie Holiday and Ella and Duke and Count Basie and Aretha Franklin had all performed.

Margaret felt utterly exhausted, utterly defeated, utterly depressed. She was utterly alone. Her feet throbbed. This wasn't the way she had imagined it at all. She must have been out of her mind to leave home. What had she been thinking?

She crossed the street and rubbed the lucky tree stump in front of the Apollo. She and Charlie were going to rub the stump together and make a wish.

"Wish you were here, Charlie," she said.

She dug out her guidebook. The Chelsea Hotel, where Mark Twain and Tennessee Williams had both stayed (and, as Dave liked to point out, where Sid Vicious had killed his girlfriend Nancy), was at the other end of town.

Margaret couldn't stomach the idea of going back into the subway. She waved at a taxi cab.

She climbed into the backseat and squinted at the driver through the thick plastic security panel. He said something to her she didn't understand. Margaret realized he must have been asking her where she wanted to go.

"It's a long story," she began. "My husband died twelve years ago ..."

She tried to explain about Charlie and the Algonquin. The driver kept interrupting. He wouldn't let her finish. All Margaret's fatigue and fear and disappointment merged into one big ball of frustration. She leaned right up to the thick plastic window separating them and yelled.

"The Chelsea Hotel, goddammit!"

The driver nodded and peeled off so abruptly that Margaret was slammed into the back of the seat.

"Oh my goodness, Charlie," she said reaching for the door handle.

That was when she noticed that her driver, who was snaking in and out of the traffic as if he were running an obstacle course, looked nothing like the picture of the man on the taxi license posted in the back with her. Margaret thought this man, who had clearly murdered the real driver, was taking her somewhere that wasn't the Chelsea Hotel, probably somewhere like a waterfront warehouse, where he would rifle her bag, take her things home to his mistress and then dispose of her.

She would have jumped out of the cab, but he was driving too fast to get out. She reached into her purse and took out a knitting needle. She knocked on the glass. "Chelsea Hotel," she yelled again, waving the needle at him.

The driver looked horrified. His wife, who wanted him to work in the bakery business with her brother, kept telling him that he would get someone like this one day. "Why can't you stay home and work in Yonkers instead of driving weirdos and drug addicts all over the city?" she had said that very morning. He sped up. When he pulled up in front of the Chelsea, both he and Margaret jumped out of the cab and started to yell for help.

After things were cleared up, Margaret checked into the Chelsea in a haze, so exhausted she didn't notice anything about the historic hotel. She went to her room and fell asleep, waking up at suppertime sweaty and disoriented. For the second time that day, she had no clue where on earth she was.

The man at the front desk told her she should eat dinner at the Venus Coffee Shop around the corner on Eighth. Margaret made her way unsteadily down the street. When she turned the corner and spotted the little café, she felt comfortable for the first time since she had left home. It had ten booths and twelve seats at the counter. It reminded her of the Maple Leaf Restaurant in Big Narrows. She ordered the roast turkey dinner with cranberry sauce and mashed potatoes. As she left, she nodded at the woman eating alone at the booth beside her. The woman, short-haired and rotund, was wearing a gray sweatshirt that said *World's Greatest Grandmother* on the front. She had ordered the turkey dinner too.

It was Wednesday night. According to her notebook, Margaret was supposed to go for a walk through Greenwich Village on Wednesday night. But Margaret didn't feel safe walking alone. Instead she sat in the small hotel lobby under a papier mâché sculpture of a fat lady on a swing and watched the people coming and going. Just as Margaret was about to go to bed, the lady from the coffee shop walked in the front door carrying a large purse and a handful of shopping bags. *She must be staying at the Chelsea too,* thought Margaret. Margaret watched her as she went by, wondering where *she* had been, all alone.

The next morning, the lady was sitting in the same booth at the Venus when Margaret arrived for breakfast. She had on a new sweatshirt. This one read *Ohio—So Much to Discover.* The woman had a map of the city spread out on her table. She was consulting a guidebook as she ate.

Margaret still had two days before the opera. She no longer knew how she was going to fill them. She wasn't tramping around this city alone, that was for sure. She wasn't getting on the subway again. Or in a taxi. The city was crazy. Maybe there was something on television she could watch.

On her way back to the hotel, Margaret walked by a woman on the corner selling something. The thin, olive-skinned woman looked about fifty. She was sitting on a milk crate with cartons stacked all around her. Margaret stopped to watch. The cartons were full of a strange oval fruit, the skins a soft blend of red and green and gold. The woman was holding a frighteningly huge knife. With a few deft strokes, she peeled the beautiful fruit, revealing its golden yellow flesh. Then she stuck it on a stick like a Popsicle and, right before Margaret's eyes, cut into the flesh five, ten times, twirling the fruit around and around on its stick. When she finished, it looked like a flower. For a moment Margaret forgot where she was. For a moment that became five minutes, and then ten, and then fifteen, Margaret stood on Eighth Avenue staring in awe at this fruit artist. She stood there until the woman made eye contact, smiled and pointed at her fruit on a stick. Margaret had to have it, wanted more than anything in the world to walk down the street eating this beautiful juicy thing—whatever it was.

"Two dollars," said the woman.

"I'm from Canada," said Margaret.

"Mexico," said the woman, pointing at her chest.

Margaret wanted to ask what the fruit was, but she was too shy. She smiled at the woman and walked away feeling adventurous. When she bit into the fruit, juice ran down her chin. It was unlike anything Margaret had ever tried. It tasted not quite like a peach but almost. Firmer than a peach. Part peach, part grape, part tropical island. It was delicious. When she got to her hotel, she still had half her fruit left. She decided to walk around the block while she finished it.

"I can do that, Charlie," she said quietly.

When she came back to the fruit lady, she bought another.

"What is this?" she asked.

"Mango," said the lady.

Margaret walked around the block in New York City all by herself eating the second mango of her life.

"I love mangoes, Charlie," she said.

On her third pass, all smiles and juice stained, Margaret put out her hand to take another fruit that the woman was handing her. This time the fruit lady wouldn't let Margaret pay. Margaret was stuffed. She didn't want to refuse, but she didn't know what to do with it.

There was a man sitting on the sidewalk by the hotel, collecting spare change. On an impulse Margaret held the mango out to him.

"Would you like this?" asked Margaret. "I'm full."

"What is it?" asked the man.

"It's a mango," said Margaret.

"Thank you," said the man, reaching out to take it. "I've always wanted to try a mango."

So this is New York, thought Margaret as she walked away. She was vibrating.

She took a deep breath and walked right by her hotel. She crossed Seventh Avenue and then Sixth and then Fifth. She had no idea where she was going. She kept looking behind her, making sure the landscape hadn't changed, making sure the city wasn't rolling up behind her, making sure there was a way back. Then she stopped checking. There was too much to look at up ahead. She saw a lacy iron sculpture of a steam shovel in Madison Square Park that reminded her of the Seal Island Bridge over the Bras d'Or, just outside of Sydney.

She cried when she came upon the statue of Gandhi striding through his little flower garden in Union Square. The city that had seemed so grimy only hours before suddenly seemed to be welcoming her. The noise that had felt so overwhelming felt overwhelmingly full of life. The people seemed friendly, not frightening.

The next morning Margaret got up and bought a mango and headed off in a different direction. By opera morning she had been all over. The East Side. The West Side. All around the town. She was so jazzed by everything she had seen that she did something on Saturday morning that surprised even her.

She was waiting for the elevator to take her up to her room when the doors opened and the woman whom she had been seeing at the Venus Coffee Shop stepped off. Today her sweatshirt read *Akron: City of Invention*. They smiled at each other, and then the woman walked towards the front door. Margaret watched her go. And then, without thinking, Margaret called her.

"Excuse me," she said.

The woman turned, and in one of the greatest acts of courage of her life Margaret said, "Excuse me. I was wondering, I have two tickets for the opera this afternoon, and I was wondering if you would like to go with me. I'm sure you have other plans, and I know you may not like opera—no one seems to—it's just I hate to see the ticket go to waste, and my husband, Charlie, was supposed to come, but he died. I mean, it's twelve years ago now. I'm so sorry to bother you. I feel foolish."

"I was just going for lunch," said the woman.

"Of course," said Margaret, turning back to the elevator.

"That's okay," said the woman, turning to the front door, then suddenly turning back again.

"Wait," said the woman, recklessly, "I would love to go to the opera. But I don't have anything to wear."

"I am sure it wouldn't matter," said Margaret. "But we have to leave in an hour. My name is Margaret. I'm from Cape Breton."

"I'm Rose. I'm from Ohio," said the woman. "What about lunch?"

"We don't want to eat before the opera," said Margaret. "People who know about these things don't eat. If you eat you get sleepy. We'll have a snack during the intermission."

"Oh," said Rose, looking anxious.

"When we get there, we'll go to the maître d' at the Grand Tier Restaurant and order something for the intermission and it will be ready for us. That's what Andrew Porter of *The New Yorker* magazine used to do. Then afterwards, we'll go to the Algonquin for supper. The Algonquin is a famous hotel. That was the plan, anyway."

They took the number nine local train to the Sixty-sixth Street station. Even in the early afternoon, the Lincoln Center was magnificent—the fountain, the two huge Chagall paintings in the windows. It was so much grander than Margaret had imagined.

And when they got their seats, there was the great gold curtain, just like the one she had imagined Doogie MacDougal bowing in front of.

As they settled into their seats, Margaret turned to Rose and said, "I was just thinking about Leonard Warren."

In the spring of 1960, Leonard Warren, who was playing Don Carlo in Verdi's *La Forza del Destino,* finished singing an aria and was just about to launch into the rousing *cabeletta* that begins "to die is a momentous thing" when he pitched face forward onto the floor and died onstage.

"Did they stop the performance?" asked Rose.

"On the spot," said Margaret.

"Did they give everyone their money back?"asked Rose.

"I don't know," said Margaret.

"My husband pitched forward to the floor," said Rose, "but he wasn't performing in an opera. He was wiping the dog's feet."

Neither of them said anything for a moment. Then Rose said, "It would have been more tasteful, don't you think, if he had been onstage."

And they both cracked up.

They had strawberries and champagne between acts.

When it was over, Rose turned to Margaret and said, "That was wonderful."

"Yes," said Margaret. Margaret hadn't felt so excited, so happy, so complete for years.

They went to the Algonquin Hotel for supper. The next morning at ten o'clock there was a knock on Margaret's door. It was Rose. She was wearing jeans and a Cleveland Indians T-shirt. She was holding a baseball hat in her hand.

"I was wondering," she said. "I have two tickets for the Yankees game this afternoon. Ralph and I were supposed to go. I wondered if you would like to come. Instead."

They sat in the sun on the first-base line, and Margaret ate peanuts and a hot dog. After the third inning, Rose went out and bought Margaret a Yankees hat. Who would think that at eighty-three years old so many new things could be happening? Who would have guessed that at eighty-three years old Margaret would be up on her feet when Jason Giambi put one out of the park?

"That was a good one," said Margaret.

And it *was* good. But what was better, what was the most wonderful thing, was that in her purse Margaret had tickets for next year's opera. For *Turandot*. She had bought them the night before, during the second intermission. What was the most wonderful thing was that next autumn she and Rose had already agreed to meet in New York, to see *Turandot* and another baseball game. And once you had tickets you had to use them. At eighty-three, Margaret had just made a friend—a war bride who lived in Dayton, Ohio.

During the seventh-inning stretch, as they stood up together, Margaret turned to Rose, little beads of perspiration on her forehead.

She said, "It's hot in the sun. It hasn't been hot like this all summer at home. It's lovely."

CARL'S RETIREMENT

In which Carl Lowbeer, a man not a little
familiar with virtue and hard work, rediscovers
a youthful desire. The only tale told in chapters.

AN AWKWARD MOMENT ON THE STOOP

On the Saturday morning of Thanksgiving weekend, Carl
Lowbeer showed up, unexpectedly, at Dave and Morley's
house just before dinner. He was wearing a flannel sports
shirt, corduroys and a blue Windbreaker. He stood on the
stoop, looking embarrassed. Carl is not the sort of person
who drops by unannounced.

Dave answered the door. Carl stared at him awkwardly.
There was a beat of silence, and then Carl and Dave
started to talk at the same time, talking over each other.
They both stopped. Then each of them motioned for the
other guy to continue.

"You," said Dave.

"No," said Carl, "you."

This went on for longer than was reasonable until Dave
finally said, "Come on in, Carl. Come in."

"I wasn't thinking of actually coming in, Dave," said Carl. "I was wondering, uh, if I might speak with Stephanie."

Carl Lowbeer, sixty-six years old. A year and a half into retirement. Civil engineer. Husband of Gerta. Carl of the sourdough starter. Carl Lowbeer calling on Stephanie, Dave's daughter.

CARL AT WORK

Carl didn't want to retire. He had watched guys around him getting ready. Jack Merryweather, for instance. Jack had a digital calendar on his desk that ran backwards, counting down the days. When you walked into Jack's office, the first thing you saw was a flashing red number: the number of days he had left. "Can't wait," he would say.

The calendar made Carl uncomfortable. Carl avoided Jack's office. Carl didn't want to think about retirement.

Jack Merryweather was building a ferroconcrete boat in his backyard. He planned to sail around the world, and damned if he didn't do it. His wife, Judy, started with him but bailed in Hawaii. Jack kept going and was in New Zealand last Carl had heard.

And then there was Greg Jones, who took up golf on his fiftieth birthday. He joined a club and even took lessons. "I hate it," said Greg to Carl one Wednesday afternoon as he headed to his lesson. "Melissa insisted I take up a hobby. Golf's the only sport I know where you're allowed to drink while you play. They seem to encourage it."

Carl had no plans for retirement. Carl's plan was to keep on working. Carl loved his work. He couldn't believe they would make him stop. He figured if he kept busy, if he *was* busy, if he was in the middle of something important, what were they going to do? *Make* him leave? The year he turned sixty-two, he started to take on projects with long timelines. He grabbed all of the onerous assignments, everything with a ridiculous due date, anything with an impossible workload.

The summer of his sixty-fourth birthday, Carl was working as hard as he had worked when he joined the company—working weekends, working nights.

When he finished his own work, he started in on other people's. One Monday, his startled secretary arrived to discover that an entire week of filing had, seemingly, filed itself. The janitor noticed that someone was using his Windex and that the garbage cans had often been emptied by the time he showed up. Louise Campbell, in public relations, wondered out loud one day if her mother was sneaking into the office at night and organizing her in-basket.

Then Carl got a phone call from Marilyn Struthers, senior manager, Human Resources.

Marilyn told him he would have to start passing files to an engineer on the fortieth floor. Carl was flabbergasted. The guy was only a kid, barely fifty years old.

"It's the law, Carl," said Marilyn.

"Hell," said Carl to Ron Peters, the VP of his division. "I can finish everything off myself in a year. Maybe eighteen months. I mean, jeez."

Ron said the same thing as that dork in personnel.

"It's the law, Carl."

Carl looked confused. Carl said, "What's the point of the law if I don't want to retire?"

Ron picked up a letter opener and started twirling it around and around. He said something about giving young people a chance.

Carl had to get out of there. He didn't want to hear this. He stood up and headed for the door, but stopped halfway across the room. He wasn't actually yelling, but it was close. "Give them a chance? Give them a chance? They don't need a chance. They've got their health. They've got their youth. Why do they need my job too?"

Carl couldn't believe it.

He didn't believe it.

He *kept* working. He was still the first person in every morning. He made the coffee and put a Post-it note on the machine with the time it had been brewed. How else would anyone know it was fresh? He figured they would change their minds. They *had* to change their minds. There was too much to do.

THE RETIREMENT PARTY

Forty years. Two months short of forty-one, if you wanted to be accurate, so you might as well call it forty-one years.

Carl would have called it forty-one if he had been in charge, but in the program it said forty. They gave him a set of golf clubs. Golf clubs. What was he supposed to do with golf clubs? He couldn't believe it.

He stood at the podium and swung the driver like a baseball club. He said, "They say golf is like life. But I don't believe that. I've watched you guys. I know it's more complicated than that.

"Jeez," he said to his wife, Gerta, under his breath, rolling his eyes as he sat down.

They made him clear out his office the next week. They didn't actually say he *had* to clear out. No one actually said *anything*. But one day a guy in blue coveralls appeared with a load of cardboard boxes and began to show him how to assemble them.

"I'm an engineer, damn it," growled Carl, grabbing the box from the guy in the coveralls.

Later that week, Norm Harrison, who was always complaining about his windowless office across the hall, poked his head in the door and said, "Do you mind if I look around?" Carl sat at his desk. Norm moved around his office as if he were buying a house. "Nice view," he said, looking over the rooftops to the park, running his hand along the edge of the desk.

"He was fondling my desk," said Carl to Gerta when he got home.

Carl came in the next weekend and went through his desk. It would have been too humiliating to do it while everyone was there. He found a brown paper bag at the back of one drawer. Inside the bag he found a little fire engine and a box of crayons. He used to keep stuff there for his kids, in case he went on an unexpected business trip and needed something to bring home.

He took the red crayon and crawled under his desk. Lying on his back, he wrote his name on the bottom of the middle drawer. *Carl Lowbeer, 1962–2002.*

THE FIRST MORNING

On his first Monday at home, Carl woke up at 6:45, as he always did. He put on a suit, as he always did. Then he came downstairs for breakfast, fixed coffee and sat there reading the paper, as he always did. He wiped the last bit of egg yolk from his plate, carried his plate to the sink and said, "Well, I have to get to it."

Gerta wasn't about to ask, Get to what? Carl took one more swallow of coffee, kissed Gerta and then, instead of heading out the back door to the garage, headed down the stairs to the basement. They had set up a desk down there. All the boxes from the office were stacked beside it.

At lunch they ate tuna sandwiches at the kitchen table. Carl said, "This is working out better than I thought. There are no interruptions. You can get so much done."

"What *are* you doing?" said Gerta.

"Getting organized," said Carl. "You know, paper clips and all that stuff. Into the right drawers. I never had time to do that before. It was always a mess."

Gerta went up to the bedroom and began to cry.

After lunch Carl took the red crayon and wrote the date on the bottom of the desk drawer. *Carl Lowbeer,* he wrote, *April 15, 2002.*

DAY TWO

At nine-thirty on Tuesday morning, Carl came upstairs and emptied the coffee maker and made a fresh batch. He put a Post-it note on the pot: *9:35,* it said.

DAY THREE

At ten-thirty on Wednesday, Gerta called downstairs. "I'm going shopping," she said. "Do you need anything?"

Carl bounded up the stairs. "I'll look after it," he said. "You relax." He took the car keys out of her hand and was gone before she could say anything.

CARROTS

By the end of the first week, Carl had taken over groceries. He would go several times a week.

At first Gerta liked the idea that Carl was doing the shopping. She had done groceries for forty years. It wasn't exactly fun.

The trouble was that Carl didn't do the cooking. The trouble was that Carl didn't know what to get. A couple of times Gerta said, "Let me make a list," and Carl got prickly. "I can do it myself," he said, as if a list would be something you would give a child.

The truth was that Carl found the grocery store bewildering. Some sections were completely overwhelming. Like yogurt, for instance. And beef. There was way too much of both. Bacon, on the other hand, was easy. He just had to find the package that Gerta always bought. Cheese was easy too. And so were carrots. Carl loved buying carrots. A carrot wasn't like a squash. You could stare at a squash and pick it up and scratch the skin and never be sure what colour the flesh would be when you cut it open. The same was true with melons. More than once Carl had stood in the fruit section staring at the melons, trying to remember which was the green one and which the orange. Carrots, on the other hand, were declarative. You couldn't make a mistake with carrots. So to play it safe, Carl always picked up a bunch of carrots.

Buying carrots on each trip would have been all right if Carl wasn't going to the store two or three times a week.

Gerta, who didn't want to discourage him, started serving carrots at lunch and supper. They ate them sliced and grated and shoestringed. They ate them roasted and sautéed. Gerta made carrot cake. She made carrot breads and carrot soup; she made carrot oatmeal cookies; she made carrot jelly. She made carrot pie and found a recipe for carrot marmalade. By Thanksgiving, Gerta had twenty-two carrot cakes in the freezer. When people dropped in,

Gerta would make them coffee and say, "Do you want a carrot with that?"

And still, there were always carrots in the fridge. Making her crazy.

CARL'S FIRST HOBBY

On the basement wall, over his desk, Carl has a large print of the Fernie train station circa 1950—a winter afternoon, blue skies and bright sunshine on new snow, the eastbound Kootenay Express stopped beside the station, a white plume of smoke rising over the Lizard range of the Rocky Mountains. Carl, born in the dying days of the steam locomotive, has always loved trains.

One night at supper—carrot ginger soup, roasted chicken with roasted winter vegetables—Gerta said, "Judith Hainline's husband, Jim, belongs to a model railroad club. There's an open house this weekend."

Carl thought, *What the hell.*

The club met in a rented warehouse in an industrial park by the airport. They had a huge layout.

"Bigger than a football field," said Carl when he came home. The railroad model had miniature neighborhoods, with a miniature downtown and a miniature industrial zone. It was a complete universe, so complicated that it took three guys to get it up and running. "Seven of us if you want to run it properly," said Jim proudly. "On schedule."

Jim walked Carl over to the table. There were cars and trucks in the streets, people walking in and out of stores, a layout that seemed to have everything—even street people, squeegee kids and a very small man picking up after his dog.

Except there weren't any trains. Or, come to think of it, train tracks, anywhere.

"Uh, where's the train?" asked Carl.

Jim smiled and kneeled down, motioning to Carl to do the same. There was a labyrinth of PVC pipe suspended under the table.

"The tracks are in the pipe," said Jim.

It wasn't so much a model train club as a model subway club.

"But you can't see it," said Carl.

"Just like the real thing," said Jim.

"Oh," said Carl.

Gerta said, "Give it a chance. You might like it."

So Carl went back the next Thursday night.

"You're on suction," said Jim.

"Suction?" said Carl.

They gave him a blue peaked hat, an orange safety vest, a wrench and a vacuum-cleaner hose. The hose was attached to an industrial-sized Shop-Vac.

"Five point five horsepower," said Jim proudly.

Jim told him that if there was a derailment, the head engineer would call for suction. Carl was supposed to hustle over with his vacuum hose, open up the pipe and suck the train to the nearest junction.

Carl nodded and wandered over to the table. He was thinking he would watch what was going on until he was needed, except there was nothing to watch.

After a few minutes, Jim came over and pointed to a bench on the far wall. "Suction man usually sits there," he said quietly.

There was a sign over the bench that read, *I SUCK*.

Carl sat on the bench for the whole night without being called on.

"I'm not going back," he said to Gerta.

"Give it another chance, " she said. "Please." There was desperation in her voice.

The next Thursday when Carl arrived, he wandered over to his bench and started to put on his orange vest. Jim shook his head and said, "Not tonight. Tonight is maintenance."

Carl brightened. Maintenance was something Carl understood. Carl said, "Dust, right?"

Jim nodded.

If you have electric trains running through a couple of miles of PVC pipe in an abandoned warehouse, you are going to get dust on the tracks.

"How do we deal with it?" asked Carl.

"Rommel," said Jim. Over by the water cooler, Gary Stevens was holding his daughter's pet rat, Rommel. Someone was spraying it with an aerosol can.

They had, explained Jim proudly, trained the rat to run through the pipes.

"What are they spraying on him?" asked Carl.

"Endust," beamed Jim.

SECOND ACT

During the next few months, Carl tried bridge, square dancing, woodworking and, inevitably, golf. None of them worked out. He began to go for walks. He would get up in the morning, put on cords and a Windbreaker and head out. He walked all over the city. He took himself downtown, wandering past shop windows, occasionally browsing in bookstores. He headed towards the lake, strolling past the marina and the rowing club. He walked through acres and acres of city parks, but as the months passed, he found himself spending more time sitting on park benches, staring into space. He felt like a ghost. He felt as if he were disappearing. *How did I get to this point?* he wondered. A year ago he had been purposeful. A year ago he had been busy all the time. Now he was unsure, unsteady, just another old man wandering around, time weighing on his hands.

Carl was full of questions. Is this all life was? Years of hard work and then petering out on a park bench? What was that song? *Old Friends. Old Friends. Sat on a park bench like …* Carl couldn't remember. What did they sit like? Wasn't there more to life than this?

He got up and started walking again. He felt … confused, questions bumping around inside his head like bees in a beehive. It had been years since he had felt like this. Decades.

Carl was born in Kitchener, Ontario, of German descent. His father was a carpenter—a cabinetmaker. He had a workshop in an old broom factory on the edge of the river, just past the bridge where the river curves. Except for a few years in the mid-sixties when he hired two men, Carl's father had worked alone. He made kitchen cabinets and windows and, from time to time, kitchen tables and wardrobes. He always had a piece of wood in his hand, a pencil behind his ear. He was always working.

Carl's mother was a chipper woman of boundless energy who lived in her kitchen. She put up jams in the spring and pickles in the fall. She baked bread all year long.

Carl could still see her in his mind's eye, leaning over the kitchen table kneading dough, strands of hair flying away from her head, flour on her apron.

"Idle hands are the devil's workshop," she would say as she greased her bread pans.

Carl had to show his mother his homework every night. If it wasn't neat enough, she made him do it over.

"If it's worth doing, it's worth doing right," she would say.

Carl worked with his father on the weekends, and every summer after grade nine. Everyone assumed that when he finished school Carl would work with his father full-time.

It was his English teacher who brought up university. The teacher showed up at Carl's home one night and had a hushed conversation with his parents. Carl was sent upstairs.

And so Carl was to be the first of his family to go to university, the first to have the privilege of an education.

But as the deadline for applying to universities loomed, Carl found himself adrift in uncertainties. He didn't know what he wanted from life. He didn't know what school he should go to or what he wanted to learn. Now that a world of possibilities was open to him, the questions seem to grow—one from another. Flipping through a university calendar one day, he came across these words in the descriptions of the philosophy courses: *Philosophy is not a theory, but an activity,* Ludwig Wittgenstein.

Carl was delighted by the notion that philosophy, questioning the world and its meaning, was an activity—something that involved energy and work.

This is what he wanted to do. He wanted to read great books of literature, he wanted to expose himself to the thoughts of writers and philosophers—he wanted time to think, to wrestle with the questions that had been plaguing him.

When he told his mother and father, they were appalled. His father had no time for riddles that had no answers.

"You have wasted too much time already in that high school of yours," said Carl's father. "Reading poetry and God knows what—that isn't work. Work is work."

His mother was clear too. Hard work was the thing that counted. "God helps those who help themselves."

School was for children. It was time to choose a profession. All this philosophic stuff was just fooling around.

Ludwig Wittgenstein had studied mechanical engineering for his first three years at university. Carl enrolled in engineering—civil engineering. The workload was heavy, but he enjoyed it. There was always some way to push yourself at school. There was always *something* to read. Something to think about. Gradually, like newspapers left out in the sun too long, all his questions faded away.

In his first five years after his degree, Carl worked out of eight different offices, in Montreal, Ottawa, Calgary and Toronto. And then he got married, and his son was born. Soon there was no time for anything but the business of living.

Carl made partner in just nine years. He was only thirty-one years old. It was unheard-of.

But here he was, some forty years later, with time on his hands, and all of those unexplored questions coming back to the surface. He was like a loaf of his mother's bread resting on the radiator. He was rising.

EPILOGUE

On Saturday morning of Thanksgiving weekend, Carl Lowbeer showed up at Dave and Morley's house just before dinner, unexpectedly. He was wearing a flannel sports shirt, corduroys, a blue Windbreaker. He stood on the stoop, looking embarrassed. Dave answered the door. Carl stared at him awkwardly. Carl is not the sort of person who drops by unannounced.

There was a beat of silence, and then Carl and Dave started to talk at once, talking over each other. They both stopped. Then each motioned for the other to continue.

"I was wondering, uh," said Carl, "if I might speak with Stephanie."

Carl Lowbeer, sixty-six years old and a half year into retirement. Civil engineer. Husband of Gerta. Carl of the sourdough starter. Carl, with a bounce in his step, looking younger and more invigorated than he had in years. Wearing a new University of Toronto Windbreaker and a Mountain Equipment Co-op backpack. Carl Lowbeer calling on Stephanie to talk about his first ever philosophy essay.

"I was wondering," he said shyly to Stephanie, a few minutes later, "if you might have any advice. I've done a lot of notes, but I'm having trouble getting started."

"I always have trouble getting started," said Stephanie. "Starting is always hard work."

"Yes it is," says Carl, a smile spreading across his face. "Yes it is."

TREE PLANTING

*Concerning a young woman and the seeds
of an obsession, and being a well-researched
story which employs an advanced literary
technique known as flashback, as well as
symbolism, similes and even the odd metaphor;
an appropriate and instructive narrative for any
reader who has fancied a life in the woods.*

Late on a golden afternoon, in the dreamy late days of
August, Dave's daughter, Stephanie, sat at a wooden
picnic table at an outdoor café not far from her dad's
record store. She was chewing on a pen, working on a
letter that she had been laboring over for a good ten
minutes. She had written two sentences. *I'm back in the
city,* she had written. *What a summer!*

She poured herself a second cup of tea, spotted two girls
walking towards her and self-consciously tucked her left
hand under the table. It was more than a month since
Stephanie had come home. Her hand still hadn't returned to
its natural shape. It remained swollen and stained, and that

was after hours of scrubbing with soap and rubbing with creams.

Stephanie was back from a summer in the woods. She had been working as a tree planter.

She had thought it was going to be a ton of fun. She had heard you could make a load of money in no time flat planting trees. So she signed up and found herself on an old school bus, heading north out of Thunder Bay in the early days of May, full of hope.

She imagined she was heading into some sort of hippie commune—a world of tents, hammocks and guitar-strumming nature-lovers. When the bus pulled into base camp, it turned out to be a burned and logged-out field of charred stumps, smudged by the smoke of a dozen camp-fires. It looked more like the battle of Passchendaele than a party: boys digging trenches, girls fighting with huge flapping blue tarps, dogs jumping around barking and everyone smoking. A large guy with a ponytail was sitting on the back of a pickup, sharpening a shovel with a file while AC/DC's "Dirty Deeds Done Dirt Cheap" blared from a speaker nailed to the top of a portable toilet.

"Wow," said the boy who stepped off the bus behind her. "This is awesome."

No one said a word to Stephanie as she wrestled her tent up. She finished just as the supper bell sounded. Before heading for the cook tent, she struggled into her new tree-planting outfit. She had bought it at Mountain Equipment Co-op—an organic cotton long-sleeved boat-neck T-shirt (avocado green), over a white tank top and a pair of convertible pants, the kind where the bottoms zip off and they turn into shorts. At supper, a boy in a plaid wool jacket that smelled of wood smoke introduced himself. "I'm Scott," he said. "I'm your foreman."

There was a meeting after dinner. Scott stood on one of the picnic tables, his long hair brushing the cage of the work light that was swinging on a yellow electric cord from the tent ceiling. Stephanie and the rest of the crew had to huddle close to hear him over the generator.

"There are three million trees to plant on this block," said Scott. "The company is paying eight cents a tree. That means there is two hundred and forty thousand dollars up for grabs. There are a hundred planters in camp, and that means each of you *should* make twenty-four hundred dollars before we move to the next block." He looked at the fifteen kids around the picnic table. "That is if we're an *average* crew. You are in the North now. And the North is the land of hard work. I want everyone on this crew to do better than average. I want you guys to plant at least twenty-five hundred trees a day."

Everyone around the table was nodding. Stephanie too. She was determined to be better than average. She was bound for tree-planting glory.

"Make it happen, guys," said Scott as he jumped off the table.

A boy with blond curly hair, wearing a bright blue Gore-Tex jacket, smiled at Stephanie. The boy's name was

Perry. It seemed he was the only guy in the camp who had come prepared. Everyone else was wearing ripped and dirty clothes. "Eddie Bauer," said Perry, pointing at his jacket.

They were supposed to be on the bus at 7:15 every morning. Before that, they were supposed to eat breakfast and make a bag lunch. By the time Stephanie got ready— no makeup (she *was,* after all, tree planting), just a good 30 SPF sunscreen, a bit of conditioning mousse to keep her flyaway hair in place and, okay, a touch of mascara—and had made it to the cook tent, all the good lunch stuff—the cheese, the hummus, the cold cuts and the bagels—was gone. She threw together a peanut butter sandwich on white bread and ran for the bus. She was five minutes late.

She sat beside a tall guy with a ponytail and a hemp necklace. His pants looked as if they were held together by duct tape. They *were,* in fact, held together by duct tape. The top half was beige. From the thighs down they were brown. He was wearing a white-collared dress shirt.

He looked like a loser. No, he looked like a totally *unprepared* loser.

Steph was wearing her new cargo pants.

Perry, the Eddie Bauer boy from the night before, was wearing orange Pumas, quick-dry pants and a dark blue denim shirt. Perry looked like a pro.

After a half-hour ride, the bus rocked to a stop on the side of a logged-out clearing. The veteran planters headed out by themselves. Scott gathered the rookies around the end of the bus.

"This is the block," he said. He was pointing at the scarred slash in the forest. From the bus, it had looked like a field. Up close, Stephanie could see it was waist high in scrub and scattered with fallen logs.

Scott said, "You each get your own piece of land."

Twenty minutes later, Scott and Stephanie were standing by the side of the road, beside a stack of plastic trays. "White pine," said Scott, pointing at the foot-high saplings.

He pointed at the alder bushes and the deadfalls and the upturned rock. "That's yours," he said.

Then he said, "The first thing is to flag your boundary so no one creams your land." He pointed at a bag of orange ribbons. "Tie one of these off every ten feet, from here back to that small rock to the right of the tree."

It was all rocks and trees as far as Stephanie could see. Before she could ask, Which small rock? Which tree? Scott said, "Make it happen, man," and was gone.

Stephanie strapped on her hip belt and clipped on three canvas tree bags. Then she tied off the first orange flag, concentrating on staying straight, determined that her boundary was going to be perfect.

It took Stephanie less than ten minutes to rip her new beige pants. She tore them as she clambered over the trunk of a fallen pine. She swore out loud. Then she broke into tears, swore again and stood there wondering what to do. There was nothing to do. Nothing but tie another flag, and then another, until suddenly and unexpectedly and mysteriously, she was back on the road. She had been concentrating so much on her perfectly tied flags that she had got herself turned around. Instead of walking in a straight line back into the bush, she had walked in the shape of a horseshoe.

It took her until eleven o'clock to flag her boundaries. By eleven, she had ripped her pants, flagged her land and eaten her lunch. She was finally ready to plant her first tree. She plunged her shovel into what looked like a nice soft piece of ground. It struck the rock cap of the Canadian Shield about six inches below the surface, the vibration ricocheting through her body.

At lunch, Perry, the boy with the Eddie Bauer jacket, walked down the road and sat beside her.

"I already ate my lunch," she said morosely.

"I ripped my new jacket," said Perry.

They climbed onto the bus at five o'clock. Stephanie fell into her seat sweaty, exhausted and starving. There was a rip in each leg of her pants. Her hands were cut and sore.

Perry fell into the seat beside her.

"I only planted five hundred," said Steph. "He must have been joking, right? No one could plant two thousand trees in a day."

"I did six hundred and fifty," said Perry. "I could have done more, but I hurt my wrist."

Stephanie didn't like that. She thought she should be able to plant as many trees as any other rookie—but surely not two thousand. Scott was exaggerating about that.

The guy with the ponytail and the white dress shirt was sitting across from them. His left hand was completely covered with duct tape, as if he were wearing a silver glove.

"How many did *you* plant?" asked Perry.

"Twenty-four hundred," said ponytail guy, unwinding the duct tape.

All Stephanie wanted was a hot shower. But by the time they made it back to camp, she was too tired to shower, too tired to do anything but eat and fall into her sleeping bag. She slept for ten hours.

She woke up at six to the sound of rain hitting the roof of her tent.

She unpacked her yellow rain gear. It had cost her $179. She had been afraid she wouldn't get a chance to use it. Perry, who sat beside her on the bus again, was wearing the same rain outfit, except in blue.

Ponytail guy was wearing the same duct-tape pants and white dress shirt.

"You're going to get soaked," said Perry.

Ponytail guy shrugged.

"You're going to get wet too," he said. He pointed at Perry's rain suit. "That thing is going to make you sweat.

And then you are going to get cold. I'll just get wet and then I'll come back to camp and I'll get dry. Rain gear is for wusses."

It rained all day. Stephanie planted 620 trees—120 more than the day before. She also ripped both legs of her yellow rainpants.

Perry planted 500, down 150 from the previous day. "I could have done more," said Perry, "but I sat in the bus for a couple of hours."

Ponytail guy planted 2,500.

The rest of that week was a complete blur. Every day was the same: up at six, stumble onto the bus and drive to the block. Every second day, the bus broke down and they had to get out and push it. One morning they had to repair a log bridge before they could cross it. Stephanie started to hate the bus and its fetid combination of sweat, abandoned sandwiches and bug spray. Most of the planters hadn't taken off their clothes since they had arrived, not even for sleeping.

As week two began, Stephanie's cargo pants were festooned with duct-tape patches. She had built her total up over the first few days but then plateaued at around one thousand.

"I did eleven hundred today," she told Perry at the end of the first week.

"I did four fifty," said Perry. "But I could have done more. I played euchre last night until dawn. I took a nap after lunch on a bed of moss. Those little bags of saplings make good pillows."

The next afternoon, Stephanie came back to her cache of trees to fill up her bags, and the trays were thrown every which way.

"They are sprayed with pesticide," Scott explained later. "That's why they smell so skunky. It was probably a bear. Bears love the smell."

One afternoon, the sky turned ominously dark and the wind came up, howling through the trees, whipping everything around, even the foot-high seedlings. When stabs of lightning began to jump out of the sky, Stephanie was so determined to push her numbers up that she just kept on planting.

And then it started to rain.

It rained for a week solid.

It wasn't just that everything got *wet,* it was that it got wet and freezing. At night, Stephanie would crawl into her sleeping bag, and it would take her hours to warm up. It seemed that as soon as she was warm, it was time to get up and put on her damp boots and her damp clothes again. One morning she woke up and it had stopped raining, but her socks were frozen solid. She put them on and slogged across the camp to the bus.

And then, after seven days of rain, she woke up and didn't hear rain on the roof of her tent. She could tell the sun was out and she could hear a group of people singing

in the cook tent. She struggled out of her bag and shim-
mied into her clothes, thinking, *At last.* She unzipped her
tent door and the brightness almost blinded her. There
was snow on the ground. At the same moment that she
saw the snow, she recognized the tune they were singing
in the cook tent. It was "Good King Wenceslas."

She thought that they would get the day off because of
the snow, but Scott made them work. She planted all day,
even though she could barely hold the little trees in her
already swollen hand, never mind get her shovel into the
earth, which was snow-covered and frozen.

People's resistance began to wear down. At night she
would lie in her tent listening to people coughing.

And then it warmed up—and the blackflies came.
Swarms of them, as if someone were pouring them out of
a giant jar. All morning Stephanie could hear Perry
swearing through the woods.

One morning Perry showed up with ski goggles and a
hat with a bug net. His shirt cuffs were taped to his wrists
with duct tape. Before he got off the bus he slathered
himself in DEET.

"They're not getting me," he said.

But the swearing was even worse.

"What was going on?" asked Stephanie when she got
back to the bus.

"They got under my goggles," said Perry, "and the
DEET melted the cable on my iPod. Then it started drip-

ping into my eyes with my sweat, and I couldn't see. I sat in the bus all afternoon."

The bugs got in your ears, up your nose, through your hair and in your eyes. The mess tent was open on the sides, so they got in your food too. You couldn't get away from them. You breathed bugs, and you ate bugs and there were bugs in your ears, so all you ever heard were bugs. Some kids tied bandanas around their ears so they couldn't hear them; some kids slathered themselves in olive oil.

The only person who didn't complain was ponytail guy.

"My name is Rob," he said.

"Why don't they bother you?" asked Stephanie.

"They do," he said. "I just don't complain."

The insides of Stephanie's arms were covered with sap, and the outsides with a rash, from constantly brushing against the trees. The pesticides on the saplings were drying out her skin, so when she opened and closed her fists, her knuckles would crack and bleed. But the thing that bothered her the most was her stubbornly low tree total. It didn't seem right that she couldn't do this—that she couldn't master something as simple as planting trees. She had always succeeded at anything if she wanted it badly enough, but she couldn't seem to crack tree planting.

She decided to try the visualization techniques she used to prepare herself for exams. She lay in her tent imagining herself planting trees really, really quickly. But when she fell asleep, she spent the night dreaming she was planting trees really, really quickly and then woke up exhausted.

Next she tried to speed herself up by listening to fast-paced dance songs on her iPod while she planted. The music made the day pass more quickly, but she suspected that her newly rhythmic movements were wasting precious tree-planting energy.

She attempted to achieve a Buddhist-like oneness with the earth, embracing the cycle of life she was helping to perpetuate. She chanted, "More trees, more trees" quietly under her breath all one morning.

When her voice gave out, she decided that she should focus on process. She was wasting too much time returning to the cache to bag up. She filled her hip bags with twice as many saplings as usual and staggered into her land. She got wedged between two trees in an unlogged section. She couldn't move backwards *or* forward. She screamed for help, over and over. What if a bear happened upon her? After half an hour, Rob showed up. He sat on the ground and laughed and laughed. Then he made her promise she would make out with him if he got her unstuck.

When she was free, she stormed off without a word. Rob knew better than to try to collect.

Stephanie was getting nowhere fast. In fact, she was going backwards. At the end of week three, the evil tree-checker woman showed up. She marked off a two-meter circle in the middle of Stephanie's land and checked the spacing of her trees. There should have been fourteen trees, all seven feet apart. There were sixteen trees. The tree-checker told Stephanie she had to replant the entire area. And she wouldn't get paid for it.

Stephanie decided Scott was giving the highballers the best land.

"I'll switch with you," said Rob. So one day she worked Rob's land and he worked hers. It didn't make a difference.

"The bugs were crazy today," said Stephanie. "Look at my hands."

"You're right," said Rob, looking out the bus window. "There are always plenty of reasons to have a bad day."

"What does *that* mean?" said Stephanie.

Things were even worse on Perry's land. Perry couldn't sleep at night, but no sooner did he get off the bus in the mornings than he was hit by a potent wave of narcolepsy. Just the sight of a pine sapling had him yawning and woozy and sneaking off for a nap. That wouldn't have been so bad, except that the planters had to pay room and board. One night after dinner, Perry did the math. "Holy crap," he shouted. "I *owe* the company money!"

The next day he borrowed a handful of caffeine pills from another planter. When everyone got off the bus at the end of the day, Perry was still wide-awake, twitchy and agitated. That night, he packed up and left camp without telling anyone. They woke up the next morning and he was gone. When they checked his land, they found he had planted two thousand trees on his last day—all of them upside down, their roots drying in the sun like hay.

They had a weekend off in Thunder Bay. Everyone spent the time showering in their motel rooms, eating in the fast-food joints, writing postcards in coffee shops or just lying in the sun. Everyone except Stephanie. Stephanie had decided that if it wasn't her focus or her process that was letting her down, it had to be her tools. She tramped around town, looking for a garage mechanic who would cut down her shovel with a blowtorch to make it lighter, sharper.

When she eventually made it back to the hotel, everyone was heading out dancing. Stephanie stayed behind to clean up and hit the sack early. She was only minutes into her shower when she discovered that the drain was clogged solid with the accumulated grit and grime of her three roommates. She scooped handfuls of wood chips and sand out of the bottom of the bathtub and then headed to bed. But the motel mattress and the clean, dry sheets felt strangely uncomfortable. At a quarter to twelve, she was still awake, sitting on the edge of the bed, staring out the window into the dark and deserted street. She watched a solitary man walking down the sidewalk, moving in and out of the shadows of the streetlamps. His head was bowed slightly, and his pace was measured and steady.

He was carrying a metal lunch pail in one hand and a yellow hard hat in the other. He was heading off to work while the rest of the city slept. The North was the land of hard work, Scott had said. Suddenly Stephanie felt exhausted. She rolled back under the blankets and fell asleep.

She was the only one who caught up on her sleep that night. And so she was the only one awake when two provincial police officers arrived at the motel the next morning.

"There have been some problems at the golf course," said one of the cops. "We suspect two of your planters."

"Why do you suspect us?" asked Stephanie.

"Someone planted ninety baby spruce trees on the eighteenth green," said the cop.

Back in the bush the next day, Stephanie still couldn't crack two thousand, even with her modified shovel.

She cornered Rob in the cook tent. "I know you aren't telling me something. There's a secret. Tell me the secret."

"Okay," he said. "I'll tell you the secret. But only if you are first on the bus in the morning."

Stephanie was on the bus ten minutes early for the first time all summer. Rob was sitting in the backseat— alone.

"Tell me," she said.

"You weren't first on the bus," he said. "I was."

She was ten minutes earlier the next morning and the same thing happened.

On the third morning, when she climbed on a half hour early and Rob grinned at her and said, "Morning," she had a tantrum.

"Okay," said Rob. "I'll tell you. The secret is … there isn't any secret."

"Of course there's a secret," said Stephanie, her voice almost hoarse with desperation. "Tell me."

"Okay," said Rob. "There is a secret. The secret to planting more trees is to plant more trees."

She thought he was making fun of her. She didn't understand he was serious.

He took her with him onto *his* land. "Watch," he said. So she sat on a huge rock, her knees drawn up to her chest, and she watched him. He took a tree from his bag with his left hand and drove his shovel into the ground. He bent over and fed the roots into the ground with the blade of his shovel. He kicked the hole shut, hardly standing up as he moved to the next spot. He didn't move fast, but he moved steadily, bobbing up and down as if he were eating the land instead of planting it. As if he were some sort of grazing animal.

She thought she had been working hard all along. Watching Rob, she wasn't so sure.

He didn't listen to music, and he didn't rest or talk to people when he bagged up. And he didn't take an hour at lunch.

He pulled a piece of paper out of his pocket and handed it to her. "I wrote this for the Internet," he said. "I posted it on a tree-planting site."

She unfolded it.

"Read it," he said.

When it is time to plant, plant. When it is time to eat, eat. Whatever you are doing ... just do it. If it's raining, you can worry about the rain all day or you can plant and make money. The rain will pass and then it will be dinner and then it will be time to go to sleep. And like the rain, the night will pass too, so better that you just shut up and sleep. As for tomorrow ... Tomorrow, read Stephanie, *doesn't even enter into it.*

Stephanie said, "I don't think I can do that."

Rob looked at her and laughed. "That's your problem," he said. "You think too much."

There are moments in people's lives that change them forever. You go into the woods to plant trees for six weeks, and you come back and your life is never the same.

Stephanie hit 1,900 trees the next morning.

The morning after that she pounded in 2,000.

Two weeks would pass before she would break the magic 2,500 mark. Before that would happen, the black-flies would return with a vengeance, and she would be bitten to bits, so swollen and scarred that everyone started to call her pizza-face. One morning she woke up and her right eye was swollen closed. She couldn't see out of it. She could have stayed in camp that day, but she used duct tape to hold her eye open and went out anyway. That was the day she pounded in 2,600 trees—her personal best.

She sat on the bus at the end of that day, sweaty and tired, sore and stinky, her pants all ripped and repaired. Her hair was filthy, her hands swollen and cut and covered with duct tape.

"Twenty-six hundred," she said. "That was awesome."

And that's what she wrote about in her letter. About the day she hit 2,600. And about the afternoon she rammed her shovel into a wasps' nest. And about how, in June, her big toe went numb from kicking at the duff and stayed numb for the rest of the summer. *It's called Christmas toe,* she wrote, *because sometimes it stays numb until Christmas.* She wrote about all that, and about the afternoon she came upon the lake at the back of her land. She came over a hill and saw the water sparkling in the sun. She couldn't believe it. She took off her clothes and jumped in, naked. Miles from nowhere. Alone in the great boreal forest. Amazed at herself. But most of all, amazed at life.

PART II

DOUBLE LIVES

SAM THE ATHLETE

A tender story, told with a light touch, from which the reader could easily infer that the author believes the seeds of victory are planted with every defeat and that the path of the heart is the only path worth following. A tale suitable for both girls and boys.

The week before school began, Sam, heading for a new school—middle school—and about to begin a whole new chapter in his life, appeared in his parents' bedroom in the middle of the night. He tapped his mother on the shoulder.

"I can't sleep," he said.

"What's the matter, sweetie?" asked Morley, who couldn't sleep herself and knew perfectly well what was the matter.

"I need new sneakers," said Sam, "for school."

Trying to decipher the fuddle between what a boy wants and what a boy needs is a game best played with hunches, with a roll of the dice and a shot in the dark. You can try to do it scientifically; you can consult the experts;

you can study the social trends and scribble notes in little files—in other words, you can do it by the book, but you'll never do as well as the mother who travels through the kingdom of boys with a purse full of rabbits' feet and chicken bones—a mother who knows the meaning of shooting stars and sneakers.

A mother who knows the difference between shoes that fit, which Sam's still did, and shoes that fit *in*.

Morley took Sam to the shoe store the next afternoon.

She was overwhelmed by the huge display of running shoes, which covered an entire wall of the store.

Sam didn't hesitate. Not for a moment. Sam knew exactly what he wanted. "That one," he said, pointing at a red runner with white wings stitched along the side.

Morley picked the shoe off the display, turned it over and furrowed her brow.

"Is it too expensive?" asked Sam fearfully.

How much is too much to make your child feel good?

Morley shrugged. "Let's see," she said.

The man from the shoe store measured Sam's feet, disappeared into the back of the store and then emerged carrying a royal blue cardboard box. The red runners were wrapped in gold tissue.

Sam sighed.

"Sit down," said the man.

Sam sat down. He watched the man pull out the first runner, unwrap it and drop the gold tissue back in the box. He watched him put the laces in the shoes.

The man smiled. He pulled the shoe open and knelt down. Sam stuck out his sock foot.

He had never felt anything like this sneaker ever before. The shoe was both tight and loose at the same time. Firm but spongy. As strong as steel, yet as soft as a sigh.

"It ... fits ... perfectly," said Sam.

"These are built for speed," said the man, who was still kneeling in front of him.

"I know," said Sam. "I can feel it."

"A lot of people find them *too* fast," said the man. "They come with a warning."

"Uh-huh," said Sam, nodding earnestly.

"Do you want to take them for a test drive?" asked the man.

Sam stood up.

"Usually," said the man, "I make people sign a waiver. But in your case ..." Sam wasn't listening. Sam was rocking from side to side.

"In your case," said the man, "I think we can overlook formalities."

Sam was eyeing the shoes in the mirror. The man waved in the general direction of the door. Sam wasn't paying attention. Sam was thinking how cool he looked. He was thinking that with these shoes on his feet, he would never walk again. He would dash and dart; he would bound and leap; he would sprint and spring.

The salesman looked at Morley. He said, "They're all wearing these ones."

Sam stepped over the empty shoebox. He walked across the store. He could feel a sense of velocity building inside him. He looked at his mother earnestly.

"These are the ones," he whispered.

He wore the shoes to the cash register. The man held up Sam's old white runners. They looked deflated, worn and tired, as if all the life had been sucked out of them.

The man asked what he wanted to do with his old shoes. Sam looked at his mother. And Morley said exactly what Sam wanted her to say. She said, "Keep the old shoes. We don't need them anymore."

When they were outside the store on the sidewalk, Morley said, "Why don't you see just how fast they are?" In his imagination, Sam didn't hear his mother's invitation. In his imagination, Sam heard the abrupt bark of a gun going off in the distance, and he was off. He cut along the sidewalk like a terrier, zigging in front of a man talking on a cell phone, zagging past a lady carrying a fancy leather briefcase. He was so preoccupied with the wind on his face, with the angle he was holding his hands so they would cut through the air with maximum efficiency, so captivated with the beauty of his new shoes, with how good his new red leather shoes with the white wings looked against the gray sidewalk, that he ran right into a telephone pole.

There was just too much to think about.

And as Sam sat on the sidewalk, his head in his hands, he was thinking that he should have known all along that the shoes weren't going to help. Middle school was going to be just as horrible as elementary school.

It wasn't that he was worried about the teachers, or the other kids, although it was partly about the teachers and partly about the other kids. Mostly it was about academics. And mostly it was about the most important academic class of them all—gym class.

Right from the beginning, gym class hadn't worked for Sam. The September he was in grade one, his teacher, Mrs. Hayes, kept talking about clothes for gym. "Don't forget your clothes for gym," she reminded everyone as they were leaving school on the first Friday. Sam looked around the class, wondering which kid was Jim and why he couldn't bring his own clothes.

Gym class was where Sam was introduced to the world of sports, and soon, all Sam wanted in the world—and he wanted it as badly as he had ever wanted anything—was to be an athlete. He kept trying so hard, and he kept failing—miserably.

He had had such hope for the red running shoes. But the running shoes weren't going to change anything. He was always going to be running into telephone poles.

His downfall had begun with his very first game of soccer. Sam loved soccer, or loved the idea of it—the idea of having teammates. The idea of the big white-and-black soccer ball, the shin guards and the high black socks, the bright red pinnie. But Sam had a huge soccer deficit. Sam didn't have the foggiest clue what was going on.

And because everyone else seemed to understand the game, Sam didn't dare ask. Instead, he developed his own soccer strategy. Sam's strategy was to stay in constant motion. He followed the pack of kids up and down the field, trying to *look* engaged but avoiding the ball at all costs. Every game he ran and ran and ran until he was so exhausted that he lost sense of everything around him. He lost sense of the field, of the kids, of the coach on the sidelines. Worst of all, he lost his sense of direction and which goal was whose. He inevitably fell behind the pack, so everyone would be running one way and Sam would be going the other. Inevitably, he would end up running full tilt into someone who was running in the right direction. Twice he was penalized for unnecessary roughness.

"He seems to be an angry boy," said Mrs. Hayes to Morley on parent-teacher night.

Baseball was even worse. Sam was banished to the outfield, doomed to watch the action miles from home plate, holding on to his mitt like a refugee clutching a battered suitcase. He would squint into the sun, praying that no one would hit the ball near him, because each time they did, Sam would automatically, involuntarily start loping towards home plate, screaming, "I got it. I got it!" And each time he was galloping in, he should have been pedaling back, because the ball had, inevitably, been hit far, not short. Sam would be coming when he should have been going, aware of his mistake too late to do anything other than make a clumsy leap in the air as the ball sailed over his head for extra bases.

When he went bowling, Sam didn't only throw gutter balls. Sam's balls actually *cleared* the gutters and bounced into the neighbouring lanes. The only time he got a strike, it happened two lanes over, and they wouldn't count it in his score.

When Murphy's dad took them curling, Sam took a mighty run and heaved his rock as hard as he could. It was going so fast that he was afraid to let go. So there was Sam, clutching the rock like a caboose, with Murphy's dad in the background, screaming frantically, "Release! Release!"

Sam sucked at sports.

He liked hockey best. But despite his years in ice hockey, and despite his mother's expert guidance, Sam never managed to master stopping on skates. He developed a method of turning in circles until he slowed down, which worked well enough, except it left him dizzy and out of the play. So, in grade five, Sam began to play goalie, thinking that with the net behind him, he wouldn't *have* to stop. He wasn't a horrible goalie. From time to time he actually made stops of sufficient improbability that his teammates skated by him and smacked his goalie pads with their sticks. That felt good. Hockey wasn't completely horrible.

And that is why, in the second week of September—his second week in his new middle school—when Sam spotted a poster outside the lunchroom, he stopped in his tracks. "Tryouts: Tuesday, 4 P.M. Field Hockey. Please wear athletic shoes and protective headgear."

"*Field* hockey!" said Sam. Hockey without skates. This, he thought, with the reckless faith of the hopeless, was the sport he had been looking for all his life. Right there, he decided he would try out.

On Tuesday of that week, Sam put on his hockey gear and joined the circle of helmeted kids waiting on the soccer field. In case it didn't work out, he hadn't told anyone what he was doing.

The coach was a short-haired, no-nonsense woman in a blue track suit.

"Let's get going," she barked. "Fullbacks, by the pitch with Aaron; halfbacks, by the bench with Chris; wings and centers, at the circle with Lee. And it looks like we finally have a goalie." Coach was smiling right at Sam. Sam was standing on the edge of the circle like a medieval knight, wrapped in his wire basket mask, hockey helmet, foam neck protector, chest protector, padded apron, leg pads and hockey gloves.

Coach reached out and put her hands on Sam's shoulders. She turned him around slowly.

She read his name off the back of his jersey. "Sam," she said. "Welcome to the team, Sam."

It was the first time anyone had welcomed Sam to a team, ever.

For the first half an hour they did calisthenics. Coach walked among them and shouted encouragement. "Come on, Lee ... lift those legs. Faster, Pat. You can do it. That's the spirit ... Samantha."

Samantha? Sam hadn't realized this was a coed team. He tried to spot the girl, Samantha, but because everyone was wearing helmets, he found it impossible.

It took about half an hour before the truth dawned on Sam. The coach was looking directly at *him* every time she had something to say to Samantha. Chris was wearing a pink T-shirt. Pat's blond hair was held back in a scrunchie. And Lee seemed to be wearing a sports bra.

And it was "Erin," the coach kept calling, not "Aaron."

"Uh-oh," said Sam under his breath.

His suspicions were confirmed at the end of practice when Coach lined the team up and handed out the team uniforms.

It was Sam's first-ever skirt.

He could, of course, have just disappeared silently. He could have slipped away and never come back to the field hockey team. No one would have been the wiser. He could have disappeared and kept quiet until he was an old man and secure in his place in the world. Then, when he was an old man, he could have told the story about his afternoon on the girls' field hockey team.

But before he could sneak away, something horrible happened, something that made sneaking away impossible. As Sam was leaving, the coach called out to him.

"Nice work, Samantha," said the coach.

Sam had been aching to hear those words ever since his first soccer game.

"Nice work, Samantha."

Well, not exactly those words. But they were close enough.

And that is why, instead of disappearing quietly as he should have done, instead of ghosting away, Sam went home instead and shaved his legs.

And so for three weeks that September, shaved-legged and skirted, Sam lived a lie.

And the trouble with living a lie, as any liar will tell you, is that day by day, your lie, which once seemed so preposterous to you, becomes less and less preposterous and more and more normal.

Almost anyone can become comfortable in a skirt.

And Sam's skirt was making him so happy—or, more to the point, he was happy when he was wearing his skirt—because, who would have guessed, after all those years, it turned out field hockey was Sam's game?

So can you blame him? Can you blame him that one night, after dinner, safe and all alone in his bedroom, Sam put his skirt on and spent an hour working out some game moves in front of his mirror?

He hadn't thought it through. He hadn't imagined what his father might think if he walked into his bedroom and found his son spinning around in front of the mirror, wearing a skirt and holding a Lady Bic razor in his hand. Sam stopped spinning, and father and son stared at each other for an unspeakably long moment.

Then they both started to speak at once, each talking over the other, and each then stopping in unison.

"Sorry," said Dave. "You go."

"No," said Sam. "You."

And there was another uncomfortable silence.

And then Sam said, "I have a secret." Sam said, "I have been living a secret life."

Dave said, "You don't have to tell me this," adding *please* under his breath. *Please don't tell me,* thought Dave.

"I have to tell you this," said Sam.

"Of course you do," said Dave. "It's okay. Tell me."

"This is hard for me," said Sam.

"Me too," said Dave.

"I have been dressing up like a girl," said Sam.

"People do that," said Dave. "Though mostly they're girls. But not always."

"It's worse," said Sam. "I have been pretending to be a girl. I have been wearing this at school."

"And you like it?" said Dave.

"Like it? I love it," said Sam. "But ..."

"You feel like you aren't being honest," said Dave.

"Exactly," said Sam.

"And you want ..." said Dave. "You want to come out ... and be honest."

"That's it exactly," said Sam.

Oh my God, thought Dave. He had never seen it coming.

Dave wanted so badly to say the right thing. This was his moment. He was at the plate, and the ball was coming towards him. This was the only chance he was going to get. He had to hit it out of the park.

"I mean, you must know that, well, Mr. Martin, for instance. I don't know if he wears skirts exactly, but he, you know, he's ... you know he lives with Phil, and we— Mommy and I—we go out with Phil and Martin some- times. And they have been to the house for dinner."

There was another long silence. The two of them stared at each other. Dave nodded, his eyes unnaturally wide. "We are okay with that," he said, pleased with himself.

Sam stared still, incredulously.

"What are you talking about?" asked Sam.

It was Morley who sorted everything out. It was Morley who phoned the school and found out that it was perfectly all right for boys to play on the field hockey team. In fact, boys and girls were allowed to play on any of the teams at Sam's new school. It was Morley who found out that Sam could go to the next field hockey game in his shorts.

And it was Morley who told him the skirt was called a kilt, and that years ago Scottish warriors wore them on the battlefields. But Sam didn't pay much attention to this. He had already decided he would keep wearing the skirt.

"Everyone on the team wears one," said Sam.

It was a good season for the team, and a great season for Sam. In the last game of the year, the championship game, with five minutes to play and Sam's team ahead by one goal, a shot came in from the wing with "goal" written all over it. It came low and hard and fast, heading for the far corner, and Sam, who was out of position, started to run. He ran and ran, and then, when he saw that he had run out of time, he launched himself at the ball, flying through the air, his blocker hand stretched out. The ball sailed towards the goal, and Sam sailed towards the ball, everyone yelling, "Get it! Get it!" And then no one was yelling anymore. The yelling stopped, and it was just Sam and the ball. He had never jumped like this in his life. Jumping and reaching and then tumbling head over heels and coming to a full stop, holding his blocker out in front of him as if the world would end if it missed the ball.

He felt the ball whack against the edge of his hand, but he couldn't see where it had gone. Then he was tumbling and rolling as a cheer roared up around him. He scrambled to his feet, backing into position, trying to see who was cheering—his team or the opposing girls.

This is the moment he will remember for the rest of his life: the moment in grade seven when he ran across the goal and jumped and fell, head over heels, and lifted his head to see *his* team cheering his save. That moment and the moment just after, when all the girls on his team, the girls from the far end of the field and the girls from the bench, were running towards *him,* whooping and screaming with delight.

When the girls got to Sam, they jumped around him, hugging him and slapping him on the back. And while they were hugging him and slapping him, Sam looked towards the sidelines and saw Mark Portnoy standing there. Mark, the big bruiser, who had teased him relentlessly over the years and caused him so much pain, looked stunned, as if suddenly the world didn't make sense. Sam will remember that too: how Mark Portnoy stared at him with an openmouthed look of disbelief and—as the girls hugged Sam—envy.

Sam had been worried about middle school. And he will be worried about high school when he gets there, too. But standing on the field on that warm spring afternoon, surrounded by his cheering teammates and watching Mark watch him, it was beginning to dawn on Sam that his future might be brighter than he had thought. Sam had always had trouble figuring out the rules, but maybe, just maybe, he wouldn't have to. Maybe, if he kept hanging in, the rules would change to suit him, and maybe, if he was lucky, the game would change too.

RENDI

A report that curiously, like at least one other in this collection passed off as humor, is brushed by longings, loneliness and a certain melancholy, which some readers might find off-putting but which the publisher hopes thoughtful souls will find edifying.

Dave's neighbor Eugene, and Eugene's wife, Maria, moved into the basement of their house several winters ago, a winter when they were already well into their eighties.

It was Eugene's idea. He thought they would be happier if they could be closer to the furnace during the long, gray winter afternoons. It turned out even better than Eugene had imagined. Before long Maria was preparing their dinners in the old basement kitchen. The next thing, they were sleeping down there.

In June, they discovered that not only was the basement warmer in the winter; it was cooler in the summer. They have been living down there ever since.

They brought down the family pictures to complete their basement home—some old sepia prints of Eugene's village in Calabria. The fearful portraits of Maria's parents. Countless photos of their son, Anthony Thomas—Tony in a crib, Tony sitting in the fig tree, Tony on skates, Tony with his wife, Tony with his own son.

Best of all, Eugene would tell you, there are fewer stairs when you live in a basement. "I don't understand," says Eugene, "why everyone doesn't live downstairs."

Eugene, who is a gardener, spends the languorous days of summer in his yard, tilting back precariously on a worn vinyl-covered kitchen chair, smoking his little Italian cigars and watching over his sweet peppers and his string beans. Tilting back under his beloved fig tree, he crushes grapes on his thighs to distract the wasps.

Eugene, who comes to life in the summer, spends the winter on a brown leather chair in the center of the big basement room where he and Maria cook and eat and doze. The television is always on down there, and the radio too. Eugene listens and watches and, more often than not, snores, all at the same time.

Eugene was in his chair the Monday before Christmas, watching a talk show on television and listening to the BBC World News, when he heard that the Italian opera singer Renata Tebaldi had died. The announcer said Tebaldi had one of the most beautiful voices of the past century. Then someone said, "She had a voice that sounded like pouring cream."

"When she sang, she sounded like pouring cream," said Eugene to Sam an hour later.

Sam, twelve years old, comes over to Eugene's house every Sunday night after supper. He brings his laptop computer with him. He sits at the big table in the center of the basement room, and Maria puts out a plate of cannoli or biscotti. Then Sam reads the emails from Eugene and Maria's son.

Thomas, as he now calls himself, lives in London. England. He moved there after finishing his university degree. Shortly after he broke the news that he would be remaining in England, he told his parents that he had been using his middle name, Thomas, since he had arrived in London. "No one calls me Tony anymore," he said.

Eugene and Maria were mystified.

"What's wrong with Tony?" Maria asked.

"Mr. Big Shot!" fumed Eugene.

Maria tried hard to make the switch, but she couldn't do it.

Eugene refused outright. But Eugene, stubborn, head-strong, set in his ways, knew that Tony was a lot like him. Although Eugene didn't understand why Tony would *want* to change his name, he also knew that once his son had made up his mind, there was nothing he could say to dissuade him.

And so while his son signs every letter and email "Love, Thomas," Eugene starts every reply "Dear Tony."

Thomas, as we'll call him, sends his parents an email every week, and most weeks pictures, too. Since Eugene and Maria don't have a computer, Thomas sends the emails to Sam, and Sam brings his laptop over and reads them out loud, using his outside voice, so Maria and Eugene can hear him. He shows them the pictures, and then Eugene and Maria yak at each other in Italian and tell Sam what they want to write back to their son.

On the Sunday before Christmas, Eugene said, "Tell him Renata Tebaldi died. Write that when she sang she sounded like pouring cream."

Then Eugene's head drooped and he began to snore softly. Sam pulled out his Game Boy, which he brings with him precisely for these moments, and got in some Pokémon until Eugene stirred and said, "Write that I want him to go back to the old country. Tell Tony that it is my dying wish that he goes back to the village where I was born."

On the other side of the room Maria snorted.

It wasn't Eugene's first dying wish. Eugene submitted his first dying wish to his son the year he turned seventy. "It is my dying wish that you return to Canada and spend Christmas with your mother," he wrote. Thomas, who had never heard his father talk like that, bought a plane ticket home that very day.

The next year, Eugene asked Thomas to find a wife. Then he asked that Thomas and his wife have a baby. Then more babies. Gradually, the wishes became, as dying wishes go, more and more peculiar.

"Please buy me some of those French chocolates when you are in Paris next."

"I wouldn't mind another Maria Callas record."

"Send three of the cotton undershirts they have at Marks & Spencer. It is my dying wish."

So, on the Sunday after Christmas, when Eugene asked Thomas to go back to the family village and said it was his dying wish, Thomas didn't pay it much heed.

Thomas had already been to Italy five times—twice to the Grand Prix in Milano, twice to a friend's villa in Tuscany and once skiing in the Alps.

"I have been to the old country," he wrote. "Why don't I send you some smoked kippers from Loch Fyne instead?"

"It is my dying wish," Eugene shot back. "How can you deny an old man his dying wish?"

This went on for several weeks until Thomas finally relented.

Eugene alerted family in Rendi that his son was coming.

A month later, on a damp Friday morning at the end of January, Thomas left Waterloo Station for the four-hour train trip to Paris Nord. He had seven hours before he left Paris Bercy for Rome, so he took a taxi to St. Germain and went to the Debauve et Gallais chocolatier. He bought a box of *pistoles,* chocolate disks with nuts. The clerk told him that *pistoles* were Marie Antoinette's favorites. "*Je sais, je sais*—I know," said Thomas.

He ate a crepe at La Samaritaine and bought a pair of mauve socks. Then he sat in the Bercy station making calls on his cell and sending emails. He took an overnight train to Rome. At Rome he changed to a train for Napoli, and in Napoli he boarded a local to Cosenza. Eugene's instructions were exhaustive. At the station in Cosenza, Thomas was to find a *country* taxi, not one of the city ones—one of the cars owned by the men who hung around the *back* of the station. Men who wouldn't charge a ransom to drive you to the mountain villages.

"I want to go to Rendi," said Thomas to the men hanging around the line of old Fiats. Thomas knew his Italian was far from perfect, but he had always found it passable in the north. The men squinted at him. The men didn't seem to understand a word.

"Rendi," said Thomas. "I want to go to Rendi."

The men looked confused. There was much gesturing back and forth. Before long, Thomas had retreated to the one word he was sure of. "Rendi," he repeated, saying the name of his father's village louder and louder until he was shouting it.

Most of the men were pointing into the mountains to the north of the station, but two of them kept shaking their heads and pointing west. Thomas took a pen and a pack of cigarettes from one of the men. He wrote the village name on the cigarette package. The men passed the package around, and there was more fast talk and much shaking of heads until a man with a red plaid shirt stepped forward, slapped his chest, said, "Rendi" and pointed at one of the rusting Fiats.

They drove for an hour, twisting up the sides of mountains, sailing through ancient vineyards and plunging into the dusty valleys. They skidded around herds of goats and bounced by old stone ruins. It was as if they were driving through time, backwards.

Thomas, sitting in the backseat, was oblivious to the sublime glory of the sunburned hills. Instead he spent the ride wondering what the stock market was doing and whether his whole life was going to be taken up by his father's wishes.

Rendi turned out to be a walled village—a cluster of red-tiled roofs on a rolling hillside surrounded by vineyards. The blue Fiat rocked to a stop at the Porta Nuovo and Thomas paid the driver and walked into town, his black leather Ralph Lauren satchel slung over his shoulder.

The first people he saw were two old ladies dressed in black, arguing at the edge of the piazza at the village center.

"I am looking for Michelina Conte," said Thomas in Italian.

The two women stared at him blankly.

"Michelina Conte?" said one woman to the other.

"*Sí,*" said Thomas. "Michelina Conte."

Thomas set his satchel on the cobblestone road. His father had told him everyone in town would know his uncle's widow.

"Il mio nome è Anthony Thomas Conte. Provengo da Toronto. Il figlio di Maria e di Eugene Conte."

Before long a crowd of people had gathered around him.

Apparently the old family connections were not as strong as Eugene wanted to think. Thomas felt sorry for his father. It seemed no one had even *heard* of Michelina Conte.

"Michelina Conte?" said Thomas as each arrived. "Michelina Conte?"

Eventually someone said, "Ahhh ... Michelina Conte."

And there was a lot of fast talk. Just like at the taxi stand, it was far too fast for Thomas to follow. And then someone ran off and came back with the priest, his black robes swaying back and forth as he swept down the street.

"Michelina Conte!" said the priest, throwing his arms around Thomas.

And so Thomas's weekend began. All the villagers pushed forward and clapped him on the back, their bewilderment dissolving. Two young men set up a long wooden table right in the center of the piazza, and slyly, like a picture developing in a darkroom tray, the wooden table began to fill with food—bottles of red wine that had no labels, a big block of hard, crumbling cheese and more. People appeared carrying loaves of crusty bread, a big dish of sweet peppers swimming in oil and garlic, a pot of bubbling tomato sauce, plates of fresh pasta.

Thomas dug out his camera and took pictures of everyone at the table. Then he gave his camera to a young boy, who took pictures of *him* with everyone. He wanted evidence to send back home.

When Thomas left Rendi the next morning, there were twenty people standing at the massive town gate waving goodbye. On the way home he wrote his father:

> I never understood before why you left Italy. Now I do. It is quaint, and not without beauty, but it is so backward. I left Canada for the same reason, and I can't imagine living there anymore. Imagine what might have become of me if you had stayed in Rendi after the war! I know it wasn't always easy for you. I am grateful for what you did.

Sam was sitting with Eugene and Maria at their kitchen table. As he read the email out loud, Eugene began to scowl. No one said anything when Sam got to the end.

After a few moments, Maria rose from the table, took their cake plates to the sink and began washing them. Eugene sat immobile. The silence was so deep and so profound that Sam glanced at Eugene to check if he had fallen asleep. When he saw that Eugene was, in fact, very awake, Sam sat and waited for the old man to speak. Finally Sam said quietly, "There are pictures."

Eugene grumbled as he hauled himself out of his chair and stood in front of the laptop.

He snorted as he squinted at the pictures. "That's not Rendi!" he said.

It was. And it wasn't. There are, it turns out, many Rendis. Rendi del mare, Rendi del castello, Rendi di Santa Maria.

Thomas had gone to the wrong one.

The indignity of his son's error provoked a dramatic and unexpected response from Eugene. With his jaw clenched and his eyes set, Eugene shuffled unwaveringly across the room and picked up the telephone. Eugene, who had never once in his life incurred long-distance charges on his own telephone—not once, not ever— Eugene, who won't even talk to his son when Thomas phones home, because he can hear the money being spent with every word—*that* Eugene, picked up the phone and dialed Thomas direct in London, as if this was something he did every day. Except it was already *night* in Canada—three in the morning in London. Maria watched with her hand on her breast.

"*Santa Madre,*" said Maria with genuine shock.

Not, however, with as much shock as Thomas. Thomas had been sound asleep when the phone rang. He picked up the receiver in a daze and heard his father bellowing at him.

When he sorted out what was happening, Thomas tried to convince his father that his memory was playing tricks on him.

"If I was in the wrong village," said Thomas, "why did they make such a fuss? They fed me. They took me into their homes."

Eugene was apoplectic. "Don't you know anything about Italians?" he barked. "They felt sorry for a man who gets himself so lost. Italians are very kind to idiots."

Then he slammed the phone down and turned to Sam.

"What are you looking at?" he said. "It's okay, it's okay. Type. Type. Tell him 'Tony, go back.'"

"What else?" asked Sam.

"Nothing else," said Eugene.

Thomas's reply arrived the following Sunday.

"Don't ask me to go back," wrote Thomas. "For God's sake, I got the point."

Eugene was shaking his head as he stared at Sam. "Write, 'What point?' Write, 'How many years in school and you talk nonsense?' Write, 'This is my dying wish.'" And with that Eugene started to snore.

Thomas went back to Italy a month later. And if I told you the progression of his second trip, it would sound to you as if in all its details it was exactly the same as his first trip. He took the train from Waterloo to Paris, and from Paris to Rome, and from Rome to Napoli. In Cosenza, he carried his black leather satchel to the back of the station and found a cab to take him to Rendi, the right one this time: Rendi in Fiore. Once again, the cab bounced over the hills and valleys of the sunburned and rocky wilderness the Italians call il Mezzogiorno. And once again, when he got to the village, Thomas tried, in his fractured Italian, to introduce himself, to no avail. Just as on his previous visit, a small group of the curious gathered around Thomas, talking so fast that Thomas had no idea what anyone was saying, until a man clenching a pipe in his mouth pushed his way to the center of the circle of people. He was wearing an overcoat and a fedora. He smiled at Thomas and said in heavily accented English, "What seems to be the problem here?"

As I said, the events of the visit were almost identical to those of the first trip.

But that is not how it felt to Thomas.

On his first afternoon in the new Rendi, Thomas was walking through one of the narrow streets when he came upon a man carrying a huge wooden toolbox. He had to step into a doorway to let the man by. As the man passed, they made eye contact and nodded at each other. Thomas had walked ten more steps in the opposite direction when something made him turn and look over his shoulder. When he did, he saw that the man with the toolbox had done the same thing. They stared at each other for what might have been an uncomfortable moment but wasn't uncomfortable at all. Then

Thomas smiled, and the man nodded again, and the moment was over. The man reminded Thomas of someone. It was only after he was out of sight that Thomas realized who the someone was. The man reminded him of himself. He was thicker and rougher to be sure, a craftsman rather than a businessman, but it could have been his own self if he had grown up here.

As the hours passed, Thomas found his head snapping around to look at one person after another. By nightfall, a feeling had settled on him. He tried to describe the feeling in an email to his father when he got home. It was an unsettling feeling, a feeling of the world shifting—a feeling of the world becoming both larger and smaller at the same time, a sense of claustrophobia and expansion all in one. He phoned his wife and tried to tell his wife about it, but he couldn't explain it to her either.

He was staying with his uncle's widow, Michelina, sleeping in a second-floor bedroom with a stone floor and a wooden shuttered window that overlooked a valley of olive trees. In the valley there were old stone arches from Roman times.

On his second morning, at breakfast, Thomas's aunt Michelina pointed at the arches and told him that when his uncle was a young man, he had a dream about the biggest arch.

"He dreamed there was a buried treasure under the far arch," she said. "When he woke up, he took an axe and a pick and a shovel and he went down there and started to dig. He dug and he dug and he dug, until he had a hole as deep as his waist. Then he hit something hard. It was a chest. He hauled the chest out of the hole and saw that the lock on the chest was already broken. And when he opened it up, the chest was empty."

Thomas said, "Someone else must have had the same dream as him. Someone else must have found the chest first and got all the gold."

And Thomas laughed and laughed, thinking to himself, *That was pretty funny*. His aunt Michelina didn't laugh. His aunt Michelina didn't even crack a smile.

She said, "That's what your uncle said."

"What happened to the chest?" asked Thomas.

Michelina shook her head. "He put a hundred lira inside and buried it for the next person who had the dream."

The sun was shining and the wind was blowing softly up the valley. Thomas and Michelina sat in the kitchen with their coffee and sweet rolls. Thomas was reminded of the quiet breakfasts he had shared with his mother as a boy, watching his father, the early riser, working in the garden while they ate their toast.

When Eugene finally dies, and that will not happen for many years yet, he will do so at home. There will be a small funeral at a local church, and everyone who attends will leave with a bottle of his homemade wine. That will be, after all, his dying wish. And after the funeral, people will go over to the house and sit in the basement room and the backyard garden and talk.

Sam will be there. It will be his first funeral. Dave will be there too, of course, and in the late afternoon Dave and Thomas will find themselves alone by Eugene's garden shed.

And Dave, who never will get to know Thomas very well, will ask him why he decided to move back to Canada from London. "It was your father's greatest wish, you know, but he would never tell that to you. I guess that's because he was an immigrant himself—because he had left Italy and never moved back, he felt he couldn't ask you to come home. He was a generous man."

Thomas will smile and reach up and tug at a branch of Eugene's beloved fig tree, and he will say, "Oh, I think he told me in his own way. A number of years ago."

Thomas will then tell Dave about the morning that he was sitting at the table with his aunt Michelina when the priest came and knocked on the door. They walked together, Thomas, Michelina and the priest in his black cassock, to the village graveyard. It was not a long walk, but it took a long time because they walked slowly, not wanting to rush the old lady. When they got to the grave-yard, they stopped before all the stones she wanted to show him. "This is my husband," she said. "This is his father, your grandfather, Anthony. This is my sister. This is her child." Thomas watched her kneel and cross herself, and he knelt beside her and did the same. As he knelt there, he peered at the photographs set in each stone, the pictures fading softly behind the cloudy glass.

He waited until she started to shift, and he reached out and helped her struggle up. They stood there for a moment more, without a word, the old lady leaning on his arm, then she waved her hand impatiently and said something he didn't hear but took to mean *enough*. He turned with her, and they headed slowly back along the sun-soaked road, back to the village where his father had been a boy.

SAM'S PREDICTIONS

Wherein we delve into Sam's past and his
future, and learn that secret fears are never
as frightful once the secrets are shared.

Every child's life is attended by a congregation of adults who teach him or her important things about this world where we live. If the child is lucky, the lessons add up, in a positive way, and the child grows to be an adventurous, outward-looking soul, a soul who trusts the universe and believes good things of the people who inhabit it.

I am not speaking here of schoolteachers or Scout leaders, hockey coaches or ballet instructors. I am talking about the pilgrims on the periphery of a child's life—men and women whom, in the best of all possible worlds, the child chooses for him- or herself. I am talking about the private relationships that parents know little or, often, absolutely nothing about.

It might be a friendship with a school janitor who offers a kind word and a smile, or moments spent with a crossing guard who takes the trouble to learn a child's name or, best, the owner of a corner store where a kid buys candy who, one day, offers the kindness of credit.

These relationships, because they belong to the child alone, are the first cautious steps into independence and adulthood.

Dave watched his son, Sam, take his first tentative steps the spring Sam was in grade four.

It was a Saturday morning in April. Dave looked out his kitchen window and spotted his aged neighbor, Eugene, reaching, wobblingly, from the top rung of an old wooden ladder, to prune the high branches of his fig tree. Dave dropped the morning paper and bolted for the back door, stopping abruptly when he spotted his son, Sam, grade four, steadying the ladder. Everything in Dave told him to get over there and take control, but in a profound moment of neighborly compassion and parental wisdom, he went back inside—knowing that Eugene already had all the help he wanted, help that wouldn't boss him around, help that would allow him to do as he pleased. Dave spent the morning peering anxiously through his kitchen window.

Morley and Dave know all about Sam's friendship with Eugene. But—and this is the important part—they don't know half of what goes on between them. Like any thoughtful son, Sam skims over most of the interesting details.

He has, for instance, neglected to tell his mother and father of the times that Eugene has offered him one of his cigars. Or a glass of homemade wine.

"I don't drink," said Sam the first time that happened.

"Too bad," said Eugene. "I am not going to be around to make it forever. It's good stuff. You might want to hurry up about changing your mind. You miss it … it's your loss."

Sam *has* tried smoking, although not one of Eugene's cigars. It was at a party, and it took an older woman to weaken his resolve. Sam was eleven. The seductress was a twelve-year-old girl from Saskatchewan. Sam left the party early, feeling sick. He quit smoking the next morning.

"It's not as hard as they say," he told his friend Murphy. "Whenever I feel like a cigarette, I eat candy."

Although they suspect that they don't know half of what goes on between Sam and Eugene, Morley and Dave approve of their friendship. But they don't know about *all* of Sam's adult friends. They don't, for instance, know a thing about Madame Nina.

Sam met Madame Nina a few summers ago. How he ended up having tea in her studio is a bit of a puzzle. Unlike endings, beginnings are often foggy affairs. But if you were looking for a beginning, you *could* say it was the summer afternoon that Sam and his best friend, Ben, were cruising around the neighborhood on their bikes, half-heartedly looking for their friend Allen. They had bought Popsicles from the store near their school and hung around the wading pool in the park and were checking out the arena when Sam said, "I bet Allen is at the park."

"We were just *at* the park," said Ben.

"I bet," said Sam.

So they went to the park.

And sure enough, this time Allen was there.

Now there was nothing that would mark *that* as an auspicious moment—not until there was an accumulation of other moments like it, and by then, of course, that first moment was long forgotten. But there were little moments like that all summer.

Sam bet Ben that it would rain the night of the corn roast—and won.

"How did you *know* that?" said Ben.

"I don't know," said Sam. "I just knew."

And later that night, the night of the corn roast, Sam won the Guess How Many Jelly Beans Are in the Jar contest.

That was when Ben said, "What is going on with you?"

And *that* was when Sam began to believe that something *was* going on.

"I don't know," said Sam. "Maybe I'm psycho."

That night, before he got into bed, Sam sat at the desk in his bedroom. It was the first time he had sat there since school had gotten out. He picked up a pencil. It felt odd to have one in his hand. He hadn't written a word for more than six weeks. He wondered if he would remember how.

He wrote the number one on the page. He stared at it for a moment; then he crumpled the page and began again.

He wrote: *Ben will call me before lunch.*

Under that he wrote the number two: *2. My mother will make me eat breakfast.*

Then, *3. Stephanie will sleep in.*

Then, almost without thinking, he wrote, *4. I will make my bed.*

He frowned.

None of what he had written seemed extraordinary enough. *Anyone* could predict any of those things. He chewed on his pencil. He bent over and he carefully wrote, *5. There will be aliens.*

The next morning when he woke up, the first thing he did was make his bed. Then he went over to his desk and put a check beside number four: *I will make my bed.*

He went downstairs. Morley was sitting at the kitchen table.

"I made my bed," said Sam.

"My goodness," said Morley. "I never would have predicted *that.*"

"Exactly," said Sam. "It's strange, isn't it?"

Morley said, "There are strawberries in the fridge for breakfast."

Sam stared at his mother deliberately. He said, "I'm not hungry."

"You're not hungry for strawberries?" said Morley. "Why don't you try a few?"

Strawberries are Sam's favorite. He went upstairs and put a check beside number two.

Ben phoned at nine-thirty.

Sam said, "I made predictions. They're all coming true."

"I'll be right over," said Ben.

Sam showed him his list.

"You made your bed?" said Ben.

"I predicted it last night," said Sam. "It was just a feeling."

"Wow," said Ben.

There was a check mark beside everything on the list, except number five.

"What do you mean?" said Ben. "Aliens."

"Aliens," said Sam. "Just aliens."

"When will they be discovered?" said Ben.

"I don't know," said Sam. "I guess today. These are today's predictions."

"How will we know?" said Ben.

Sam frowned. Sam said, "Maybe it will be in the newspaper."

And so they headed for the door, the two of them standing as they pedaled their bikes around the corner, swaying left and right, heading for Snyder's. They were about to do something that they had never even *considered* doing before. They were about to buy a newspaper.

They locked their bikes together and ran into the store.

Mr. Snyder was standing where he always stood, behind the fogged glass counter at the front, a cigar clamped in mouth. The boys bumped into each other as they bounced past him, moving to the long wall of magazines with the newspapers fanned out on the shelf beneath them. There were newspapers from all around the world: from New York and Boston, Washington and Paris, London and Rome.

Sam and Ben studied the front pages carefully.

"Holeee," said Ben.

There it was, plain as day, splashed across the top of *USA Today*: U.S. Campaign Aims to Stop Illegal Aliens.

"Why would they want to *stop* them?" said Ben. "Aliens are so cool."

A moment later, when they were standing on the sidewalk astride their bikes, Ben said, "We should phone the police."

"I didn't do anything wrong," said Sam uncertainly.

"I know," said Ben. "You could *help* them. You could predict where the bodies are."

"What bodies?" said Sam.

"The missing bodies," said Ben. "That's what police do. They look for the missing bodies."

Sam was beginning to feel anxious.

The days of that summer chunked by like telephone poles along a country road, as if they would go on forever.

As July folded into August, Sam's powers seemed to be growing. He predicted Ben would get a bike for his birthday, and he did. He predicted that the Blue Jays would rally and win a game they were losing by seven runs, and sure enough, they came from behind in the ninth.

"Geesh," said Ben, "it's so weird."

By the time September snuck up on them—by the time the first day of school leapt off the kitchen calendar, landing on them like a cat on a mouse—word of Sam's special powers had spread. Not everyone believed in them, of course. But some kids did. Some kids believed that if Sam predicted something, it was *guaranteed* to come true.

Gregory Hannover believed.

Gregory cornered Sam and Ben one afternoon as they were walking home from school, their backpacks hanging from their shoulders.

"Predict that I'll pass spelling tomorrow," demanded Gregory. "I never pass spelling."

"That's because you never study," said Ben.

"That's why I want him to predict that I am going to pass," snapped Gregory, staring at Sam, suddenly all serious.

Sam stared back. Ben was watching like a corner man at a fight.

"What's the big deal?" said Gregory. "Just predict."

"I predict ...," said Sam slowly. "I predict ...," said Sam, furrowing his brow, thinking about it. "I predict that you are going to study."

"Huh?" said Gregory. "I can't study—I always get distracted."

"It's my prediction," said Sam.

Gregory caught up to Sam the next morning at recess. "You were right," he said breathlessly. "It happened. I studied. I know the words. It's weird."

"I know," said Sam.

That afternoon, after school, Geoff Braymore came up to Sam and Ben on the ball field.

"Can he predict how tall I am going to be?" Geoff asked Ben.

"What?" said Sam.

"Can you predict that I will be six feet tall?" said Geoff.

"I can't do that," said Sam. "It would be unethical."

Geoff was the shortest kid in the class.

"Well, how about five ten?" said Geoff. "Would that be so unethical?"

And then Deirdre Simpson cornered Sam. Deirdre, with her curly brown hair and her pink jean jacket. Deirdre, who always smelled like a basket of exotic fruit, got Sam all alone and said, "I have a problem."

Sam shrugged.

Deirdre said, "There's a boy I like. I want to kiss him."

Sam said, "So?"

Deirdre said, "Can you predict that I will kiss him?"

"Okay," Sam said, shrugging. "What's his name?"

Deirdre said, "His name is You."

"Me?" said Sam.

"Yes," said Deirdre. "You." Deirdre's eyes were closed. Deirdre was leaning softly towards him.

Sam looked around to see if anyone was watching.

He leaned forward. His lips brushed her ear.

"I predict," he said softly, "that I won't." Then he ran.

When Sam's predicting had started, it had been fun. It had been the summer, and it was just Sam and Ben, and it was something to do. Then it had gotten serious, making Sam feel full of power and promise.

But now he wasn't feeling powerful; he was feeling overwhelmed. Things were getting out of control. He had barely escaped being kissed.

That night, alone in the windless dark of his bedroom, a harrowing thought occurred to him. Maybe it wasn't a game. Maybe he *was* psycho. Maybe he wasn't *predicting* things that would happen—maybe he was *causing* things to happen.

The thought terrified him.

A waterfall of horrible possibilities cascaded through Sam's imagination: his mother was sick, his dog was dying, his father was going away and would never return. His mind was moving so fast he couldn't sleep.

Ten o'clock became eleven o'clock; eleven turned to twelve. Now all he could imagine were fearful, awful things, and he was convinced that if he kept thinking them, they would all come true. He tried to focus on happy times.

He remembered the greatest afternoon of his life—the afternoon his father had appeared at his classroom and said, "Sam has to be excused from school. Sam has a doctor's appointment." Sam was nervous because he didn't know about the doctor. He thought maybe he was so sick that his parents hadn't wanted to tell him. But instead of driving to the doctor, his dad winked and headed downtown. He was taking Sam to his first-ever ball game.

Sam tried to concentrate on the glory of that afternoon.

They sat on the third-base line, and his dad bought him a hot dog and a pop from a man who walked among the seats. He tried to remember the man with the hot dogs. He could almost hear him coming towards them, but when he turned to look, it wasn't the man, it was Deirdre Simpson, smiling and waving at him. Gregory Hannover was standing beside her, and he was spelling something out loud over and over: *k-i-s-s-i-n-g.*

Sam met Madame Nina the next afternoon, after school.

It was Ben who had discovered her storefront studio. He showed Sam one August afternoon. They had stood on the sidewalk straddling their bikes as they read Madame Nina's sandwich board: *Discover Your Future. Palmistry, Tarot, Aura: 25, 40, 60 dollars.*

Ben had said, "We could set up a booth at the fall fair. I could be your manager. We could make *serious* money."

As they stood and stared, a woman wearing jeans and a ball cap came out and picked up the sandwich board and took it inside.

"That was her," said Ben.

"She didn't look so special," said Sam.

"Neither do you," said Ben.

And now Sam was standing outside Madame Nina's storefront, knocking on her door, his nervousness about the unknown washed away by the tide of fears from the night before.

"Hello," said Madame Nina to the boy standing at her door in the sweatshirt and ball cap.

"I have to talk to you," said Sam.

"Well, then, you must come in," said Madame Nina.

Sam followed her into her tiny studio. It was no bigger than his bedroom. There were two chairs and a table. Madame Nina was pointing at the chairs. Sam chose the one closest to the door. The walls were covered in dark red fabric. There were two paintings of the moon, and complicated charts of the stars. There were candles flickering. It was like being in a tent.

"Now," said Madame Nina, sitting down across from Sam, "what can I do for *you*?"

Sam shrugged.

Madame Nina said, "You look like a boy who has a lot on his mind."

Sam started to cry.

Madame Nina wasn't used to little boys knocking on her door, but she was used to tears. She handed Sam a box of Kleenex and waited.

And that is how Sam met Nina Cheroldi—that September afternoon that he went to her studio and sat in the chair by the door and started to cry.

He told her everything. How he had discovered his gift in the summer, and what had happened at school. He told her he thought he was psycho and that he was scared that if he thought bad things, maybe they would happen.

She waited for him to finish and then she smiled and handed him a large deck of cards. She said, "Do you know how to shuffle?"

Sam shook his head, "No."

"Just mix them up a bit, like this," she said. "These are the tarot," she said. "Do you know anything about the tarot?"

Sam shook his head again.

"Good," she said. "No one does." She took the cards from him and squared up the deck.

She began to lay the cards faceup on the table.

"Are you ready?" she said.

Sam shook his head again.

"What?" said Madame Nina.

Sam said, "You have to teach me the rules. I don't know how to play."

"The only rule," said Madame Nina, "is that you must listen to what the cards say." Then she said, "Look at all these hearts. You feel things deeply for such a young man."

Sam nodded. "Yes," he said.

"And you worry," said Madame Nina.

Sam nodded again. "Sometimes," he said. Then he yawned.

"Sometimes," said Madame Nina, "you worry so much that you have trouble sleeping."

"Yes," said Sam quietly. "Sometimes that happens."

Then Sam said, "How do you stand it?"

"Stand what?" said Madame Nina.

"Knowing what is going to happen," said Sam.

She said, "No one knows what is going to happen, Sam." She nodded at the cards.

"Not even these cards," she said. "But if you listen carefully to people, if you listen carefully and with all of your heart, they will tell you what they *want*. And what *you* want is to know that everything is going to be all right. And it will be—everything is always all right in the end."

"Really?" said Sam.

Madame Nina looked at her watch. "Always," she said.

"Oh," said Sam.

Then he said, "I have one more question."

Madame Nina nodded.

"What if it isn't?" said Sam.

"What if what isn't?" said Madame Nina.

"What if everything doesn't work out well in the end?" asked Sam.

"Ah," said Madame Nina. "That's easy. If it doesn't work out well in the end, that means it's not the end."

"Oh," said Sam.

When he got home, Sam told his mother he was going to make a prediction.

"I predict I am not going to make my bed anymore," he said.

A year went by before he saw Madame Nina again. And then, after that time, another year. And then it turned into an annual ritual. Sam goes to see her every September before school starts. He sits at the table, and she does his cards. Every September, Madame Nina will do Sam's tarot. He won't tell his parents until the year Madame Nina moves. Then, one perfect summer morning, when the wind is soft, Sam and Morley will drive by the storefront where her studio used to be, and Sam will say, "There was a lady who had a place there, and I used to go there some-times and talk to her. She was nice."

And Morley will look at him and say, "When?"

And he will tell her the whole story.

And that will be the end. But that won't be for years yet.

PART III

LIES AND

BETRAYAL

KENNY WONG'S PRACTICAL JOKES

A lengthy story, replete with both deception and good humor but nevertheless containing some weighty ideas that would be hard to miss. Easier to follow and considerably more fun than anything written by several bestselling authors who spring to mind.

Kenny Wong jumped out of bed early on the last Saturday in March. He got up, dressed and bolted out the back door without stopping for coffee or anything. He was a full three hours ahead of his normal Saturday routine.

Kenny jumped into the car and drove to a nearby mall. He bought the Saturday paper at a convenience store, and then he strode across the mall's parking lot to a doughnut shop, whistling. He bought a coffee, sat down and spread the paper in front of him. He flipped to the want ads. To *Objects for Sale*. He was looking for the ad he had carefully dictated over the telephone on Wednesday morning.

And there it was. When he spotted it, Kenny beamed and slapped the table so hard that his coffee overflowed the cardboard cup, drenching the sports section. Kenny was so excited he didn't notice.

Big Bucks Polka, read the ad. Kenny slapped the table again. He looked as if he were going to burst. *Record collector will pay top dollars for Walter Ostanek and any or all polka albums. One day only. Bring your records Monday morning to Dave's Polka Palace (formerly the Vinyl Cafe). No calls. No Early Birds. Get top cash on the spot.*

Kenny closed his eyes and grinned. He was imagining some guy in lederhosen jostling for position out front of Dave's store on Monday. Monday, April first. April Fools' Day. Kenny wasn't sure he could wait.

He folded the want-ad section and stood up, leaving his half-full coffee and the rest of the paper behind him. He reached into his pocket and dropped a toonie beside the paper—the first time he had ever left a tip in a doughnut shop. Ever.

On the way to the car, Kenny started thinking about last year.

Last year on April Fools' Day, Kenny called the police from a phone booth and told them, anonymously, that he had just been passed, for the *second* time in a week, a phony twenty-dollar bill at a local record store. Just before the cops arrived, *Dave* received a call, from a voice that he recognized but couldn't place, reminding him that it was April Fools'.

"Your friend Kenny Wong has hired a couple of university students and dressed them up as cops," said the caller. "They're going to accuse you of passing phony money. You might want to give them a rough time."

When the two detectives wandered into Dave's store and started asking questions, Dave breezily admitted to passing phony twenties. "I print them at home," he said, offhandedly. "I'm surprised it took you so long to turn up."

He carried on like this for a good ten minutes. When the puzzled cops suggested he come with them to the station, Dave laughed in their faces. He told them it was time for them to go back to school. "You aren't dealing with an amateur," he said.

The cops called for backup. It took four of them to bundle Dave into the back of a squad car.

"Aren't you guys going a little far with this?" asked Dave when they cuffed him.

It took a good part of the night to straighten things out.

Last year was good.

But this year was going to be better.

It isn't a one-way street. Kenny Wong runs a little restaurant down the block from Dave's second-hand record store—Wong's Scottish Meat Pies. If you asked either of them, neither Kenny nor Dave could tell you exactly when this April Fools' business began.

But they would tell you that one April, Dave got into Kenny's café in the middle of the night and replaced the gravy powder Kenny uses for poutine and hot turkey sandwiches with chocolate pudding mix. No one in the kitchen noticed anything until the cook splattered some of the chocolate gravy on the rim of a plate, wiped it with his thumb and then absentmindedly brought his thumb to his mouth. That wasn't until late in the afternoon.

As soon as he could, Kenny rewound his cash-register tape and found, to his horror, that they had already sold seven hot chocolate–turkey sandwiches. The disturbing part was that no one had complained.

There was the year Dave got a mechanic friend to rewire Kenny's car so the horn blew every time Kenny put his foot on the brake. In his wildest dreams Dave hadn't imagined Kenny would edge up behind a policeman at the very first red light he struck.

After three blasts from Kenny's horn, the cop burst out of his car, smoke steaming out his ears.

To someone like Dave, who came of age on a tour bus with some of the wildest groups in rock and roll, all these gags are pretty tame stuff. But they bring back memories of his misspent youth, and for that alone, they are worth the minor inconvenience of a night in jail.

For Kenny, the annual pranks are an echo of a different kind—a reflection of a flame lit when he was a boy, growing up in Alberta.

Kenny grew up in the town of Burnt Creek. His father, Henry Wong, was the majority shareholder of the Half Moon Cafe. The Half Moon is no more. Someone bought it out in the seventies, removed the old Formica booths and tore out the counter, with its twelve high stools. It is now called the Bamboo Terrace, and it has an oversized menu with color photos. But it is in the same building, just across the bridge, next door to where the old hotel used to be, where the tracks used to cross Railroad Street.

A moon-faced man who liked to smile, Kenny's father built a reputation for honesty in Burnt Creek. In the fifties, CPR linemen, who would leave for work before seven and wouldn't make it back until after dark, would leave their paychecks with Kenny's father to cash or deposit at the credit union—the same service Kenny's grandfather used to perform for local ranchers, who often had to leave town before they got their checks from the cattle sales.

Kenny and his brothers grew up in the Half Moon. Their mother would march them into the restaurant every night, and they would eat supper together at a table in the kitchen.

All the Wong kids had jobs to do in the café before they started school. Kenny's first job was cutting the butter pats with the metal butter slicer that was kept on a table in the pantry, where Old Man Chu, skinny as a broom, used to peel potatoes and carrots and drop them into a bucket of water. The September Kenny was five, the

September he went to kindergarten, he was given the added responsibility of filling the miniature ceramic coffee creamers. Kenny would come into the restaurant at seven-thirty, after his bowl of Sunny Boy cereal, and sit at the counter with all the round-topped jugs arranged in front of him. He would earnestly fill each one, right to the top, and then slide off his stool and carry the creamers, one by one, behind the counter. He would line them up beside the Jell-O and the slices of pie on the glass shelf above the celadon green milkshake machine.

In 1949, the year Kenny turned five, the Wongs were the only Chinese family in Burnt Creek.

His first week at school, a group of girls from grade two surrounded him at recess and chanted, "Chinese, Japanese, look at your dirty knees."

Henry, trusted by the linemen and the ranchers with their paychecks, was never accepted by the businessmen of Burnt Creek. He wasn't asked to join the Elks or the Rotary until 1976. He was never invited to the Businessmen's Association meetings, and when the Chinese were finally given the right to vote in Canada in 1947, not one of the candidates asked him for a donation or asked to put a sign in his café window.

The only person who got under his skin, however, was Eddie Kawolicks. Eddie ran Kawolicks's Menswear, *Where Sharp Men Shop*.

Eddie came to the Half Moon for lunch every Friday. He would sit in the same booth each week, right in the middle of the restaurant, and order "Chickee Flied Lice." He always did this loud enough that everyone in the place was sure to hear him. When he got his meal, Eddie would eat a few mouthfuls, then put his fork down and say, "This sure is good chickee."

Sometimes he would call Henry, who was usually up in the front somewhere, maybe serving coffee or cashing someone out. "Hey, Henry," he'd call. "I haven't seen my cat for a few days. You haven't seen the cat, have you?" He would then look around the Half Moon at everyone and laugh out loud.

At other times, Eddie Kawolicks would stand by the cash register at the end of his meal with a toothpick bouncing in his mouth and say, "I would come for lunch every day, Henry, but if I ate that much rice I'm afraid my eyes would go slanty."

It bothered Henry Wong that he didn't speak good Canadian English. He felt humiliated when Eddie Kawolicks made fun of the way he talked. And it was tiresome having to ignore all of the insults and bad jokes.

One Friday night when he was twelve, Kenny asked his father why he didn't refuse to serve Eddie Kawolicks. "You should tell him he's not welcome."

Henry Wong was sitting at the dining-room table counting the day's receipts when his son said that. He didn't stop counting. He said, "I don't want to offend other customers."

He didn't look up, but he sensed his son's shoulders sag.

It was snowing that night when Henry went back to the Half Moon to close. When he came home, everyone was already in bed. He shook Kenny awake. He told him to get dressed. They drove back to the café in silence. It was late. They were the only car on the main street, their tire tracks rolling silently behind them into the snowy darkness. Henry parked in the alley, and they went in the back door through the kitchen and into the dark café.

The only light was the yellow and red glow from the big Wurlitzer at the front. Henry pointed at the booth where Eddie Kawolicks always sat. Kenny sat down. He watched his father walk to the front where the cigarettes were kept in a scratched glass case. He watched him reach up to a high shelf.

Henry Wong brought a carved wooden box the size of a pound of butter to the booth where his son was sitting. Eddie Kawolick's booth. Then Henry walked into the pantry and came back with a candle and a stick of sandlewood incense. He sat down on the bench opposite his son, opened the wooden box and unwrapped a piece of bright yellow silk. Kenny leaned forward and saw three old round coins with square holes in the middle, lying on the silk. His heart was beating fast. He knew what was happening. His father was going to consult the Sage.

Henry Wong had never thrown the I Ching with his son before. Kenny knew, without his father saying anything, that they were going to ask the Sage about Eddie Kawolicks.

They sat quietly for five minutes. Then Henry wrote something in a small black book, using the Chinese characters that Kenny never learned. When he had finished, Henry picked up the three coins and held them in the palm of his hand so the orange flicker of the candle lit them, the smoke from the incense curling around. Six times he dropped the coins. Each time Henry examined their faces and marked what he saw in his book.

When he finished, he looked across the table and spoke to his son for the first time since he had woken him.

"Huan," he said. "Wind over water."

"What does it mean?" asked Kenny.

Kenny's father stood up and got a teapot and two bowls.

He poured them each a bowl of tea.

"The Sage says there is a harshness present."

He leaned down and blew across the top of his tea. Little black waves lapped at the edge of the bowl.

"The Sage says if you hold a hatred against someone, you become bound to that person. To free yourself from the binding, you must be forgiving. We must forgive Mr. Kawolicks."

Kenny looked disappointed. "I don't think the Sage has ever been to Burnt Creek," he said.

Henry Wong looked at his boy with wonder. He brought the bowl of tea to his lips and slurped at it.

"If we are going to do something, Wing Kin, we must be like the summer wind over the water. We must be so gentle that Mr. Kawolicks does not even feel the breath of the wind on his face."

Then Kenny's father stood and walked into the kitchen. He came back with a cardboard box. It was full of little glass jars—jars of paints and coloured inks. He took out a small, pointed paintbrush.

"Watch carefully, Wing Kin," he said.

There was a painting hanging on the café wall at the end of the booth, the booth where Eddie Kawolicks sat, where his father had just thrown the coins of the I Ching. It was a painting of a lake in a forest. Kenny had never looked at the painting carefully.

His father reached up and took the painting off the wall. He pointed to the far end of the lake. There was a figure standing on a rock. The figure was very small, smaller than Kenny's fingernail. Kenny leaned forward and squinted in the candlelight. He had never noticed it before. It was a young woman—a girl, maybe. She wasn't wearing any clothes. She was bending at the waist, with her feet in the water, her breasts in the sun.

"He looks at the girl," said Henry, gesturing with his paintbrush. Kenny watched his father unscrew a glass jar of blue paint. He watched him set the black lid upside down on the top of the table and dip his brush in the dark ink. And then he watched him paint a bathing suit on the girl who was wearing no clothes and standing by the lake.

"Now," said Henry putting the painting back on the wall. "It is time to go home."

The next Friday, Henry saw Eddie Kawolicks frowning at the painting of the girl.

Henry waited two weeks. After two weeks had passed, he added fluffy white clouds into the blue sky and a shadow over the girl in the bathing suit by the lake. Two weeks after that he painted a sweater on the girl.

Slowly, over a period of weeks, the gentle wind blew more clouds over the lake in the painting, and the white clouds turned to gray and the leaves started to rustle on the trees. And then, ever so slowly, the leaves began to change color as the season of the painting turned gradually, imperceptibly, from summer to autumn.

Henry brought out his box of inks and paints on Thursday nights when everyone had left for the day, even Old Man Chu, who peeled potatoes and carrots in the pantry. And then, when he had finished with the painting, Henry Wong removed the bench from the booth where Eddie Kawolicks sat and replaced it with a bench that he kept at the back of the kitchen, a bench that Henry carefully shaved a quarter of an inch off each week, so that each week the seat moved closer to the floor. Every Friday when he arrrived for lunch, Eddie Kawolicks would slip lower and lower, and the top of the table would move up his chest, like tea being poured into a bowl. After six months, the table was so high that Eddie Kawolicks looked like a little child when he sat in his booth. He was becoming uncomfortable in this restaurant where he used to hold court.

"We are making him into a little man," said Henry to Kenny one afternoon. "Soon he will blow away."

Each Friday, having shortened the bench, Henry increased, by a spoonful or two, the amount of food he put on Eddie Kawolicks's plate.

It was just a spoonful or two each time, but as the weeks went by, the spoonfuls added up, and soon Eddie was struggling to finish the plate of fried rice that he used to eat with such gusto. One Friday, when Henry set the plate in front of him, Eddie pointed at it and said, "Is the rice going bad or something? You giving it away?"

"How I make a living giving food away?" said Henry dismissively, his arms crossed.

The girl in the painting was now standing beside a frozen lake in the winter. Eddie turned to look at the painting and then back at Henry. He seemed pained. He started to say something, but he stopped. He shook his head and shifted uncomfortably. The table was halfway up his chest. He looked like a little boy.

As the weeks went by, Eddie became more and more fidgety. He couldn't get comfortable. He sat in the booth, shifting his weight back and forth. Two Fridays in a row he splattered soy sauce down the front of his shirt. And then he knocked over his water.

One Friday, he was able to eat only half the food on his plate.

The next Friday, he didn't show up. And that was the last of him.

"You see, Wing Kin," said Henry, "he has become so small that the Sage blew him away."

Kenny moved to the city in 1972. When he arrived, he was carrying his father's instructions to look up Ross McGregor—one of the CPR linemen whose paycheck Henry used to deposit in the credit union. McGregor had lost his job with the railroad years before, and Henry had helped him out with a small loan.

McGregor, with the help of the loan and an old family recipe for meat pie, had opened a small café. He was ready to retire when Kenny showed up, and, as a gesture of gratitude to Henry Wong, offered to sell his café to Kenny. In those days it was still called McGregor's Scottish Meat Pies. When Kenny took over, he didn't change a thing for five years. Then one day it occurred to him that he had earned the right to have his own name on his business and, with McGregor's approval, he painted over McGregor's name and added his own. He was still selling mostly meat pies in those days. He added a few Chinese dishes to please a regular customer who, having received bad news about his cholesterol and seeing what Kenny cooked for himself, asked if he couldn't try some. Gradually, and without any conscious planning, Kenny added more Chinese dishes—things he remembered his father serving in the Half Moon: beef and green pepper, barbecued pork, fried rock cod, ginger and chicken.

Some years ago he put up a sign in the front window that is still there. It says, *Sorry, we are out of meat pies.* But he has still kept the same name. Wong's Scottish Meat Pies.

When he retired and sold the Half Moon, Kenny's father used to come to the city to visit his son every fall. He liked to sit at one of the round tables at the back and sip tea, smoke and read the paper the way Old Man Tong, the most infamous gambler in Alberta, used to do in the back of the Half Moon in the forties and fifties.

One day when Henry was visiting, Dave came in for lunch and sat down with him. Kenny was hovering around, and then he sat down. His father said something in Chinese, and Kenny pointed at a painting on the wall— a painting of a young girl holding a pair of skis beside a frozen lake. "My father asked if you knew the story of the painting," he said.

Dave looked at Kenny and then at Henry, who was grinning and nodding his head.

And that's when Kenny told him about Eddie Kawolicks and how they had blown him out of the Half Moon, and they all laughed. And then Kenny told about the time he had put Kool-Aid crystals in the shower head before his mother had her mah-jong club over. It was one of those lunches that went on and on. Dave told them about the night they had filled the bathtub in some roadside motel with blue clothes dye and lowered the bass player from Question Mark and the Mysterians into the tub while he slept. And how the bass player carefully poured alcohol into the grout of the tiles in the bathroom where Dave was staying two nights later, hid in the cupboard until Dave was sitting on the toilet, and then opened the door and lit the grout on fire.

They told these stories and laughed until they nearly choked. It was the next year on April Fools' that Dave got into Wong's Meat Pies at night for the first time. This was back in the days before Dave or Kenny had kids—before Kenny had renovated, even—and there was still indoor-outdoor carpet on the restaurant floor. Dave soaked the carpet with water and scattered cress seed around. This was on a Friday night, so the seeds had all weekend to germinate. By Monday, when Kenny opened up the café, the floor was a carpet of sprouted cress, and there was a sheep tied to the front booth, grazing contentedly. That was the start of it.

So a few weeks ago, on April first, when Dave arrived at the Vinyl Cafe and saw the professionally painted banner hanging over his storefront declaring, in bold red letters, *Dave's Polka Palace,* he laughed, but he wasn't surprised. He stopped before he crossed the street and took in the tableau: the new sign and the ten people waiting. They had been there long enough that they had begun going through each other's records and were trading. When Dave finally crossed and unlocked the store, they were so caught up with one another that they didn't even notice him. One soft, doughy-eyed man in a cardigan seemed to be the center of attention. He was buying everything he could get his hands on.

Dave was as polite as he could be and bought a little of what came, some of it simply because the people seemed so pleased to have a place to bring it. But there was surprisingly little to buy, thanks to the man in the sweater. And that night, on Monday, April first, on the way home, he stopped in at Kenny's for a coffee.

"Heard you had a big day," said Kenny.

"Yeah," said Dave. "I just wanted to say thanks."

Dave put down his coffee and reached into his pocket.

"It pains me to do this," he said, "but I thought it only fair."

He handed Kenny an envelope.

Kenny took the envelope and opened it. It contained two crisp fifty-dollar bills.

"What's this for?" he asked.

"That ad," said Dave. "That was very funny. But it actually brought in a couple of very valuable records. I think I just had the biggest day I have ever had. I thought you deserved a finder's fee."

Kenny Wong frowned.

The newspaper ad had cost him forty dollars—but he had paid four hundred dollars for the banner.

He started to say, "Exactly how much did you make?" But he stopped himself and looked at Dave carefully.

"Wait a minute," he said. He was about to say, You're just yanking my chain, aren't you?

Instead he looked at his friend and said, "You aren't going to tell me. You'll never tell me."

"Now what," said Dave, smiling innocently, "do you mean by that?"

THE HAIRDRESSER

*Wherein Morley remembers that honesty
is always the best policy, and Dave learns
something he already knew.*

For the past twenty years, Morley, faithful beyond fault, has gone to the same hairdresser whenever she needs her hair cut.

Morley goes to Lawrence. She discovered him when she and Dave moved into the neighborhood where they still live. A woman who has her priorities straight, Morley discovered Lawrence before she found a doctor or a dentist. And over the past twenty-odd years, Morley has followed Lawrence from one salon to the next.

Right from the start, Lawrence made Morley feel special. Instead of delegating the job to an assistant, Lawrence washed Morley's hair himself. He kept a special bottle of shampoo for her and used it instead of the salon's regular rehydrating, mineralizing, oxygenating, detangling, protein-boosting, volumizing apricot shampoo with the jojoba infusion.

If there is one thing in the world that Morley hates, it's a jojoba infusion. Lawrence remembers things like that.

In fact, Lawrence's memory may be the most appealing thing about Lawrence. He remembers how his clients take their coffee, and details about their families. "How was Sam's party?" he might ask if Morley showed up after Sam's birthday. Morley felt she and Lawrence had a special rapport, a relationship built on the important things of life—like history, trust and jojoba.

Over the past few years, however, things have been changing—slowly, slightly, but significantly nevertheless. Over the past few years, Lawrence has begun to let things slide.

One afternoon, as she settled into his chair, Lawrence brought Morley a cup of tea instead of coffee. Another day he used the foul-smelling jojoba-infused apricot shampoo and would have finished off with hairspray if Morley hadn't stopped him.

Not the end of the world, to be sure—more a disappointment than a disaster. And Morley, faithful beyond fault, resigned herself to the changing and slightly diminished Lawrence, to the way things were now rather than the way they used to be. It had been years since Lawrence had asked her what she wanted done to her hair or suggested a cut he thought would make her look good.

She had noticed it, but she hadn't given it much thought until the Saturday morning she went to get her hair cut and came face to face with the salon's new stylist, a young hairdresser from Quebec with a liquid accent and spiky black hair.

His name was Mathieu. And he had taken over the chair right beside Lawrence—although when Morley walked in, he was everywhere except the chair: jumping around the room, brandishing his scissors in the air, trying to persuade the woman he was working on to let him loose on her head.

"What's the worst thing that can happen?" he called over his shoulder as he blew past Morley with his hands full of magazines.

"If you don't like what I do, we'll change it." Then he dropped to his knees in front of his chair. "Please. I am begging," he said. "You were born to be blond."

As the hour passed, Morley, watching Mathieu from Lawrence's chair, felt as if she were watching from somewhere in Kansas. As if Mathieu were in Oz.

That was the day that Lawrence told her he had been thinking of opening a salon for dogs. He was waving his hands around, staring at Morley in the mirror, not looking at her hair at all. "Do you know how much you can charge for styling a poodle?" he asked earnestly.

Morley was telling Betty Schellenberger all about it when Betty called on Sunday night.

Dave and Morley had just finished dinner. Dave was lying on the couch reading a comic—the latest installment of *Clyde Fans*.

Morley was moving around the kitchen, unloading the dishwasher, wiping counters and talking to Betty on the portable phone.

She was telling Betty all about Mathieu and what a riot he was. That discussion, of course, led her to Lawrence, and how he had been letting her down.

"Twenty-one years," Morley was saying. "We have been together for almost twenty-one years."

Twenty-one years? thought Dave. *It's been twenty-three.*

Dave, out of sight but not out of earshot, overheard Morley on the phone in the kitchen and assumed she was talking about him.

"He irritates me," said Morley. "He doesn't listen to me anymore."

How was Dave to know that Morley was talking about her hairdresser?

"We don't have anything new to say to each other anymore," said Morley in the kitchen. "We have said it all."

Dave propped himself up on the couch.

"It used to be so much fun," said Morley in the kitchen. "I never imagined it could get so … I don't know … boring."

Okay.

Dave shouldn't have been listening in. But he was listening. And he was thunderstruck by what he was overhearing.

"Everything is so businesslike. He assumes he knows what I like. Even when I ask for something different, he doesn't pay attention."

Uh-oh.

"It feels like he is just going through the motions. He won't even look me in the eye. He just looks in the mirror."

Good Lord.

"It used to take an hour," Morley was saying. "Now he speeds through it in fifteen minutes."

Holy cow.

Morley. His sweet wife. His partner of twenty-three years. His soul mate. The mother of his children. His rock.

It felt as if his head were going to spin right off his shoulders.

What had he done wrong?

When had this started?

What mirror?

And what was she saying now? Oh my God. She was saying, "There is this other guy. I would love to try him out. Just, you know, once, maybe."

Dave leapt off the couch and stood in the middle of the living room. His heart was pounding. He had to do something and he had to do it fast. He stood there trying to figure out what.

Morley said goodbye to Betty and headed upstairs. Dave watched her go and, without an inkling of what he was doing, bounded up the stairs behind her. Morley was standing in the bathroom, gazing in the mirror. She was thinking, *My hair always looks the same. I always look the same. I'll never be a babe.*

She didn't notice Dave standing behind her when she picked up her toothbrush. Dave was looking over her shoulder at her reflection in the bathroom mirror as she brushed her teeth.

"Oh, hi," she said. Then she stopped and turned and said, "Do you think loyalty is an important quality?"

"What?" said Dave, trying to ignore the ringing in his ears.

"If you're in a bad relationship," said Morley, "should you stay in it out of loyalty?" She dropped her toothbrush in the glass on the sink. "I always thought loyalty was admirable," she said, "but life is so short." And without waiting for an answer, she pushed by him and fell into bed.

Morley went to asleep immediately, snoring softly and twitching. She dreamed that she was having her hair cut. Lawrence was using dog clippers. When he finished, he gave her a Milk-Bone and charged her twice the normal amount. She tried to complain, but all she could do was bark.

Dave tossed and turned all night. By morning he had worked himself into a complete panic.

The next morning he felt as if he had woken up in a different time zone. He felt jet-lagged. He couldn't concentrate. He couldn't sit still. All day he paced around his store, aimlessly cruising the aisles, shuffling and straightening albums in their bins, tinkering with signs.

He went to his friend Kenny Wong's café for lunch. He sat at the counter and fiddled with his water. "I'm not really hungry," he said, getting up to leave. He ordered a bowl of soup but barely touched it.

He finally fessed up.

"I think Morley is seeing someone else," he said.

"Don't be crazy," said Kenny. "Morley would never do that."

Dave looked at Kenny forlornly.

"Phone me if she starts behaving suspiciously," suggested Kenny.

"Suspiciously?" said Dave. "Like what?"

"Buying new clothes, changing her hairstyle. That sort of thing. It's classic."

As April folded into May, Morley couldn't stop thinking about Mathieu. And the more she thought about him, the more she yearned for a different haircut. Every day without Mathieu became a bad hair day. By the end of May, Morley could barely stand to brush her hair.

Morley thought about Mathieu for another month, and then on a Wednesday afternoon, Lawrence's regular day off, Morley phoned the salon and asked if they could fit her in for a style.

"Just a style," she said. "Not a cut. I'm not ready for a cut."

"Mathieu's had a cancellation at four," said the girl on the phone. "What's your name?"

"Helen," said Morley, giving the girl her mother's name.

She wore a baseball hat and sunglasses to the salon and slinked passed the receptionist and shampoo girl.

"Actually, I'm Morley," she said to Mathieu when she made it to his chair. "I made an appointment for my mother, but she couldn't come. I didn't want it to go to waste."

She went with her layered bob, intending to let Mathieu wash and style it and nothing more, but he stood behind her, held up her hair from the back and let it fall through his fingers like sand. Over and over, he picked up her hair and let it drop back to her shoulders piece by piece. Then he said, "I have to cut this."

She had known this was coming. It was inevitable. If she didn't want him to cut it, why had she come?

"Okay," she said quietly.

He sent her off to be shampooed. When she returned to his chair, Mathieu gently draped a nylon cape around her shoulders and began to draw his comb through her hair. There was an intensity to his actions: each stroke of the comb, each clip of the scissors, was measured and deliberate. Mathieu's eyes never left her head. As Morley watched him in the mirror, she was transfixed, almost overwhelmed, by his attention. When he was finished, Morley finally looked at herself. She looked totally different. Smarter. More sophisticated.

"I love it," she said.

She felt exuberant.

She couldn't wait for Dave to come home.

So she dropped in at the store instead.

"What do you think?" she said. "I decided it was time for a change."

"Don't panic," said Kenny Wong to Dave when Dave burst into his restaurant ten minutes later. "Make a fuss. Win her back."

And so Dave set off to woo his wife. As he was packing up for the day, he picked up one of his all-time favorite LPs from the bin where he keeps the blues, a bin marked *She Never Loved You Anyway*. The album was Junior Wells's *Hoodoo Man Blues,* a classic from the Delmark label.

On the way home, he decided to up the ante. He bought Morley a green Jane Jetson Pez dispenser—Morley had always loved the Jetsons. He added a pack of refills at the counter. *What the heck,* he thought.

Morley smiled when he gave her the Pez, and gave him a little hug. But she left the album on the dining-room table while she made dinner. Dave didn't think his presents had made enough of an effect.

"What about flowers?" asked Kenny Wong.

So the next day, after work, Dave went to the florist. He couldn't believe his luck. They had Venus flytraps.

Each day he brought home something different.

"Ever since Mathieu cut my hair, Dave's been bringing me little treats," Morley told Betty. "It's so cute."

"A Venus flytrap?" asked Betty doubtfully.

"Yes," said Morley. "And a pair of wool socks. And a bouquet of Tootsie Pops—all red."

Morley loved the sudden attention, and she loved her new hairstyle. But she was also plagued with guilt. She had to change her route to work so that she didn't go past the salon and accidentally bump into Lawrence. And one evening, when she saw him in the grocery store, she had to abandon her basket and bolt.

"I've got to stop this," she told Betty. "I can't keep seeing Mathieu like this."

But she went again. On a Wednesday—a Wednesday afternoon in September.

"I'll need three hours," said Mathieu. "I want to add some color."

Morley, who had never even had highlights, was reluctant.

"I don't know," she said.

"Trust me," said Mathieu. "You'll love it."

While Morley was sitting in the salon chair, guilty, nervous and excited, Dave was slumped behind the counter in his record store staring at the piece of paper he had found on the kitchen table that morning.

There were three words on it, written in Morley's hand. *Mathieu—2 P.M.*

Dave was staring at the paper and reaching for the phone. He was about to call Betty Schellenberger.

It had taken him all day to screw up the courage to make the call. If anyone knew what was going on, Betty Schellenberger would. Betty was like a liaison officer for the neighborhood. She collected every scrap of information she could get her hands on and disseminated it to those in need. If you had to know what time the community-center Christmas potluck started, you rang Betty. If you needed to find a reliable babysitter, Betty had the names. And if you wanted to find out whose large dog was leaving the mess in your front yard, Betty was likely to point you in the right direction. If anyone knew Morley's private business—or, more accurately, if anyone would *share* Morley's private business—it would be Betty Schellenberger.

"Betty," said Dave, getting right to the point. "Do you know about ... Mathieu?"

"Of course," said Betty. "It's not exactly a secret."

"She hasn't told me," said Dave.

"Well, Dave," said Betty. "It's not something you would necessarily share with your husband, is it? I have a date with him, too. I haven't told Bernie."

"You're seeing him too?" said Dave, incredulous.

"Yes," said Betty. "I'm seeing him right after Morley."

Dave's mouth was so dry his tongue was sticking to his teeth. "Where?" said Dave. "Where is she meeting him?"

"At his place, of course."

"Give me the address," said Dave with sudden resolve.

Morley's transformation had already begun as Dave bolted from his record store. She had been shampooed and towel-dried, and Mathieu had worked on her with his scissors for fifteen minutes. "Just a shape," he said. Now, while Dave flew down the street, Mathieu was fiddling with a small dish of hair color, a shade he had mixed specially for Morley.

Dave was checking numbers as he ran, without thinking about what he was doing or what he was going to do when he got to wherever it was he was going. He was just consumed by the need to act. When he found the right number, he burst through the salon door without registering where he was or what was going on around him. He spotted Morley before he spotted anything else. His wife, Morley—a black nylon cape cinched tightly around her neck, half her head covered in clumps of hair, the other half festooned with dozens of little pieces of tinfoil, something red dribbling down the side of her face—had never looked worse. He had never loved her more.

"Morley," he blurted out, "I love you. Don't go through with this. It's not too late!"

Everything in the salon screeched to a halt. As it did, Dave slowly took in his surroundings: the women sitting in the chairs, the stylists with their hairdryers poised in midair, the spiky-haired young man with his mouth gaping open, hovering over Morley with a paintbrush in his hand.

All things considered, the salon staff were very nice to Dave. They guided him to a quiet corner and a soft chair. They brought him a coffee. And he sat and he waited, and after the coloring was finished, he and Morley walked home together.

"I told him I wanted something natural," said Morley as they walked along.

"It *is* natural," said Dave, pointing at the bright red leaves on the maple tree in the park.

They sat on a park bench, and Dave, overcome with love and relief, finally asked the question he had been afraid to ask before he knew the answer.

"Are you still happy with me?" he asked. "Is everything okay?"

Morley, with her licorice red streaks, looked at him and said, "I would tell you if it wasn't."

And so it was that six weeks later, Morley called the salon and booked an appointment with Lawrence. Before she went, she phoned Lawrence himself.

"I feel a little embarrassed about this," she said. And she told him everything.

She told him about the day he brought her tea instead of coffee, and about the time he used the apricot shampoo. And about Mathieu.

Lawrence was a little chilly the first time she had another appointment with him, but she didn't let him get away with it. "We have to try something different," she said. "And it has to be your idea."

"I was thinking," he said, "that we could start with apricot shampoo."

That's when she knew they were going to be all right.

And she isn't wrong. They will be all right, although it will take longer than she thinks. Lawrence will suggest things, and they will try them, but not many of the things will work. Morley was never meant to have dreadlocks. Or to be blond.

But it won't be what they are doing that counts—just that they are trying new things and that they are working on them together.

As for Dave, Dave will realize that sometimes a little uncertainty is not such a bad thing in a relationship, that courting shouldn't end with marriage. He will keep bringing Morley stuff—root-beer-flavored jelly beans and sponge toffee. And on her birthday, instead of going out to one of the neighborhood restaurants they favor, Dave will cook for Morley this year, just the way he did when they were dating—a cheddar-cheese hot dog in the toaster oven and s'mores over the gas flame of the stove.

DAD IS DYING

A flawed, cautionary tale about the dangers of mendacity, which even the editor mistook to be about the dangers of living with dogs. Not without a certain pathos which, given the confusion, could be felt as easily for the author as for the protagonist.

Most people will tell you that spring is the most reassuring of seasons. There is something about the renewal of the natural world—the return of the sun, of the songbirds, of God's green garden—that puts a spring into many lives.

Not Dave's life, however. Spring always settles uncomfortably around Dave. It comes with the echoes of school exams, endless rain and unexpected snowstorms.

Even now it comes uncomfortably. Another spring—another year older. Again this year, as the days lengthened, Dave began to feel listless. All Dave saw in the light of spring were new wrinkles. The wrinkles made him worry. The worry made his stomach ache. He lost his appetite. He felt faint. Before long he was engulfed in a full-blown hypochondriacal funk. He was checking his pulse obsessively, sneaking away to take his temperature every few hours.

"You're fine," said Morley.

He didn't feel fine. And neither did Morley. An unexpected flurry of budget problems at work meant she was unexpectedly busy. She was so busy, in fact, that this spring Morley had no time for her garden, no time for her family and no time for herself. The only time she saw her neighbors was as she flew past them in her car.

As May rolled into June, Morley was feeling a loss of connection with everything that mattered to her.

It was Sam who stirred the wind that filled his parents' sails and pushed them out of the torpor of this heavy spring. But the wind that he stirred—the wind that would rescue his mother and father—almost shipwrecked him.

Like all storms, no one noticed its first stirrings. It began one morning at breakfast. Sam came downstairs and found his father backing out the door with Arthur, the dog, in his arms. Arthur was looking limp and pretty much dead.

"What's the matter with Arthur?" said Sam. Sam was standing on the bottom stair, dead-still himself—except for his heart. His heart was pounding. Morley was moving through the kitchen, grabbing her stuff: her purse, her briefcase, her keys. Where were her keys? She'd had them just a moment ago.

"Dave, where are my keys?"

Dave, turning to answer, whacked Arthur's head against the door frame.

"The keys are in your hand," he said.

Morley looked down at her keys and screwed her eyes shut. Sam, still standing on the stairs, still motionless, said it again. "What's the matter with Arthur?"

Morley, who was collecting her lunch now, didn't stop to look at Sam when she said, "I don't know, sweetie. I'm taking him to the vet."

It was one of those moments that begged for a time-out. One of those moments when Morley should have stopped, a moment when she should have taken some time with her son. She knew this even as she was trying to stuff her lunch into her briefcase.

Stop. Stop. Slow down, her heart was saying. *Stop,* said her heart, waving a red flag of warning. *Late,* said her head. *No time to stop. Go, go, go. You can deal with this later.* Morley had been counting on getting to work early. She hadn't been planning on a run to the vet. But there was Dave coming back through the door.

"I started the car," he said, kissing her forehead. "He's in the back."

"Is he going to die?" said Sam.

"Sweetie," said Morley, from across the room, "he's getting old. He's going to die someday."

That was when it began. That was when the wind began to feather the water of Sam's life. Sam was standing on the bottom stair in his red Spider-Man sweatshirt, his jeans creeping up his legs, his hair uncombed, his sneakers undone. He was staring at his mother as she was going out the front door. But this was just the first stirring. It was two hours later that the breeze settled in.

It was in English class. Mrs. Estabrooks asked Sam to read out loud, and Sam started to cry—not out-loud sobbing, but there were tears running down both cheeks.

Mrs. Estabrooks said, "Sam, what's wrong?" Sam tried to say, My dog is sick, but instead a waffly snort came out of his mouth—or out of his nose, more accurately.

He snuffled and wiped his eyes. By then everyone in the class was staring at him. People in the front were twisting in their chairs to get a good look—Mark Portnoy smirking, Sam's friend Murphy looking horrified. All eyes were on him and he was crying, plain as day. Sam thought, *I am too old to be crying about a sick dog.* So he began to edit. He stared at Mrs. Estabrooks, his bottom lip quivering, making no sound as he tried words out in his mind. *My dog is dying,* he tried. *No. My dog died.* He still hadn't said anything. He was sitting and staring at Mrs. Estabrooks, and she was staring back at him.

"Sam?" she said.

Sam bit his bottom lip and stood up.

That was the beginning.

Everyone stared at Sam as he looked down at his shoes and said, "My dad is dying."

Word spread like wildfire. By the middle of the afternoon, everyone had heard.

The wind hit Morley almost as soon as she got home. She hadn't been in the house for more than ten minutes when the doorbell rang. Morley was surprised to see Mary Turlington standing on the stoop. Before either of them said anything, Mary burst into tears.

"Mary, what is it?" asked Morley as she led her into the kitchen and sat her down.

Mary was wiping her eyes, thinking, *Damn, damn, damn. Get a grip,* she thought. *This isn't the time to come apart.* Mary pulled herself together and looked at Morley and said, "Oh, Morley, I just heard." And she burst into tears again.

Morley had just got off the phone with the vet and had herself just heard the concerning news about Arthur. She had been thinking it through, trying to process it, trying to be philosophical, when the doorbell had rung. Now she looked across the table at her friend. "Mary," she said, "it's not for sure yet. They did some tests, but they don't have results yet ... and even if he isn't ... even if he doesn't ... you know ... Mary, he's getting old anyway."

"What?" said Mary.

"I can never figure out his age," said Morley. "You take the year and multiply it by seven. Don't you?"

Mary said, "For God's sake, Morley. He's two years older than you."

Morley wasn't listening. She was still talking. "They age faster than us, right? I mean, they don't live nearly as long."

Mary thought, *I have to stay calm. My friend is losing it, and I have to stay calm.* Morley, who had always been the Rock of Gibraltar, was coming apart in front of her. And why shouldn't she come apart? She had a right.

"Anyway," said Morley standing up, walking over to the fridge. "However you look at it, he *is* getting old." She had taken out a bunch of carrots. "Mary," she said, "I knew he wasn't going to last forever."

Morley brought the carrots to the table and sat down. She took a knife and began to cut the greens off the carrots. Morley was not busying herself with carrots because she *needed* to cut carrots. Morley was doing it because she was worried about Mary. Mary seemed fragile, as if she was going to start crying again. Morley was thinking that some sort of activity in the kitchen—the sight of someone getting food ready, cutting carrots—might distract her, calm her down.

"Quite frankly," said Morley, standing up and carrying the handful of carrots to the sink. "Quite frankly," said Morley, "I'm okay with it. I think it's going to be harder on the kids. I think the kids are closer to him than I am. It's understandable. For all intents and purposes, he's been around all of their lives. I mean"—she picked up the vegetable peeler and she tapped it against her forehead—"he has. Hasn't he?"

Mary looked at Morley. She was peeling the carrots as if she didn't have a care in the world.

"Quite frankly," Morley continued, "it hasn't been easy over the past few months. He's dropping hair all over the place. He's shedding, Mary. And he has started to drool. And that's not the worst. I tell you one thing I won't miss—his breath. Honest to God, sometimes he smells like something you'd find at the back of the fridge."

"Oh my God," said Mary.

"To be perfectly honest," said Morley, handing Mary a peeled carrot, "if I had a choice, I'm not sure I would do it again."

Sam was late getting home that afternoon. On the way from school, Murphy and Sam had gone to Snyder's for ice cream.

"Give him more," whispered Murphy to the girl fixing Sam's cone. "His dad is dying."

The girl handed Sam the biggest ice-cream cone ever. And she wouldn't take his money.

Neighbors started showing up at Dave's record store the next morning. Carl Lowbeer was first. Dave didn't see him come in. Dave had been taking his pulse.

"Hey," said Carl.

Carl was standing by the door, next to the stuffed gorilla. Sixteen years, he and Dave had lived in the same neighborhood, sixteen years of street corners and dinner parties. Twice when the Lowbeers went overseas, Dave had babysat Carl's sourdough starter. Yet despite all that history, Carl had never been in Dave's store. Not once. And there he was.

"Hey," said Carl.

"Hey, Carl," said Dave.

"Hey," said Carl again. He was still standing by the door. "Hey," said Carl for a third time. "You look ... great, Dave."

"I don't feel so good," said Dave.

Carl hadn't moved.

"I'm not contagious," said Dave. "You can come in."

"Oh God," said Carl as he rushed up to the counter. "I wasn't thinking *that,* Dave." Carl stared at Dave intently. "No. Really," said Carl, looking right into Dave's eyes. "You look like you are doing okay."

Dave's stomach was aching again. Carl was holding a little package under his arm.

"Really," said Carl. "You look great."

They both noticed Carl's package at the same time.

"Hey," said Carl.

He put the package on the counter beside the fishbowl of record centers. He pushed it towards Dave and nodded his head encouragingly.

"It's for you."

Dave opened the package. It was a glass bottle of green powder.

"Blue-green algae," said Carl, beaming. "Our immortal ancestor, Dave. There are more nutrients packed into that little jar than in any food known to man. There's a lot of power in that jar, Dave."

Carl was nodding his head vigorously, agreeing with himself.

"God bless you, Dave," said Carl. Then he turned and left. Actually, he turned and bolted.

Dave phoned Morley.

"Carl Lowbeer was just here. He gave us a jar of ..." Dave held the jar up and read the label to himself. "*Spir-u-lina*. He gave us a jar of spirulina."

There was a long pause. Then Dave said, "Me neither. But you might know it by its other name: pond scum."

That morning at Sam's school, announcements included a moment of silence for those who were struggling with illness. Sam, his head bowed and his eyes closed, could feel the weight of his classmates' stares. Everyone knew the morning thought was for him.

On Sam's way out of the classroom at lunch, Mrs. Estabrooks touched his head affectionately—a sort of pat. Sam saw Mark Portnoy watching. He pulled away and ran his hand through his hair, mussing it. Rubbing off the teacher germs.

On his way home, Sam went to Snyder's again. He waited for the same girl, and then he stood in front of her, trying to look sad, his head hanging.

"I don't know what I want," he said glumly. "*Nothing* really appeals to me anymore."

He walked out of Snyder's with a bigger cone than the day before. He almost walked right into Doreen Lamb-Stilwell. Doreen, a notorious gossip, had made it her business to be there to bump into Sam. It had taken Doreen only a day to work out that Sam was going to be a more reliable source of information than his mother, who—Doreen was happy to tell anyone who asked—seemed a bit cavalier about the whole thing.

"If he bites the biscuit," Morley had said to Doreen that morning, "I think I'll get a new one. And the sooner the better. It'll help the kids cope with the loss."

It was just after breakfast. Doreen had come over with a frozen vegetable lasagna. Morley was tidying up the kitchen, putting dishes in the dishwasher.

"But this time," she said, juggling a stack of dirty plates, "I am going to get a younger one. They're easier to train when they're younger."

Morley bent over and put a pot in the dishwasher. Then she stood up and looked out the backyard window.

"And," she said, "I'm not going to make the same mistakes I made this time. The new one is not sleeping in the bedroom. I can't stand the snoring."

The phone rang.

"Excuse me," said Morley.

"One thing for sure," said Morley coming back to the table a few seconds later, "I am going to make sure the new one is fixed."

"Sam," said Doreen Lamb-Stilwell in front of Snyder's. "Sam, I am going to ask you some difficult questions. I need to know these things so I'll know how I can help."

Sam nodded earnestly while he ate his ice cream.

"Sam," said Doreen, "are there headaches?"

Yes, nodded Sam, licking his cone.

"Nausea?"

Yes, he nodded again.

"Vomiting?"

Sam, who hadn't spoken a word, continued to nod while he chased ice-cream drips with his tongue.

"Is there incontinence?"

Sam didn't know what incontinence was. He took a break from the ice cream.

"Yes, exactly," said Sam. "It's the painful kind," he added. Sam couldn't help himself. Once he started he couldn't stop. "And you never know when it is going to come," he said. "Sometimes in the car. Sometimes at supper."

"Oh my God," said Doreen.

The vet called that night. She wanted to keep Arthur over the weekend. She had tried a few things and wanted to see how he made out.

Morley met Bernie Schellenberger the next morning on the sidewalk, in front of the house. Bernie was carrying a three-cheese lasagna. Morley was fiddling with the car door, fumbling with her keys and bracing her briefcase against the car with a knee.

"Morley," said Bernie, "I just heard."

"Oh, thanks, Bernie," said Morley over her shoulder. She was still struggling with the lock. "It's okay. I am trying to look on the bright side."

"The bright side?" said Bernie. "I didn't know there was a bright side."

"We haven't got the final word, but they say it should be resolved by the summer. One way or the other."

There. The door was unlocked.

"We'd been talking about going away," she said, "but you know Dave ... there's always something."

Morley pulled the key out of the lock. She released her knee, and her briefcase fell to the ground, her wallet tumbling out. Change spilled every which way. She knelt down. Bernie knelt beside her.

"Here," he said, holding out three coins.

"Thanks," said Morley, reaching for a quarter. Then she paused and looked directly into Bernie's eyes. "I just don't want him to linger. You know. It would be such a drag if this went on and on and screwed up the vacation. I've been thinking if it comes to that, I'll just put him down. That sounds awful, doesn't it?"

"Well," said Bernie, "I guess that would sort of be Dave's decision, wouldn't it?"

"I think I'd have as much say as Dave," said Morley. "You know what a suck he is, Bernie. I mean, if things were getting difficult, I might just go ahead and arrange it, without telling him. You know—he wouldn't have to know."

"I don't think you can do that, Morley," said Bernie. "I think there's a consent thing, isn't there?"

"Oh, Bernie," said Morley, reaching out and touching his arm. "For God's sake—loosen up. Things have changed. Men don't get all the say anymore."

"But wouldn't that be … murder?" said Bernie, pulling away from her.

Did Morley detect fear in his voice?

"You can't just kill without asking," said Bernie. "Can you?"

It *was* fear.

"Who are we going to ask?" said Morley. "The dog? Do you want the dog's consent? I suppose it could *technically* be murder. But when the road in front of you is so clear and it is nothing but suffering …" Morley shrugged.

"I don't know, Morley," said Bernie coolly.

"They have shots, Bernie," said Morley. "It's not painful."

On Saturday, Sam was invited to sleep over at Murphy's house.

"How's your dad?" asked Murphy's mom. It was far safer asking Sam than asking Morley. Morley obviously didn't want to talk about it. Some people did, some people didn't—it was her right.

Murphy's mom had talked with Morley when she had picked Sam up and dropped off a spinach lasagna.

"How is he?" she had said to Morley quietly, earnestly.

"Who?" said Morley.

"Your ... husband," said Murphy's mom, immediately wishing she hadn't opened her mouth.

"Dave?" said Morley, waving her hand dismissively. How was Dave? Dave who that very morning had dropped an open can of sardines on the kitchen rug?

"Sometimes," said Morley, "he just gets to be too much."

Murphy's mom wasn't going to ask Morley again. But Sam didn't seem to mind. Sam seemed unusually comfortable with it. That's because ever since word had got out that Dave was sick, Sam had been living the life of Riley— free ice cream, sleepovers ... On Sunday the Turlingtons were taking him to a baseball game. There had been a few moments of awkwardness, like the morning thought at school, but all in all, Sam wasn't suffering.

Sam's suffering started on Monday. It began innocuously enough, on the front steps of the school. Jordy, a boy in grade two, was waiting there for Sam. Jordy was holding his mother's hand. When Sam approached them, Jordy's mother pushed the little boy forward.

"Jordy has something he wants to give you, Sam," she said.

Jordy handed Sam a plastic bag. There was a wild mushroom lasagna and a book in the bag. The book was called *Comfort in the Arms of the Angels*.

Sam looked at the book and then at Jordy's mother. Jordy's mother started to cry.

"Oh dear," she said, wiping her eyes. "Oh dear," she said again. Then she picked up her son and ran away, leaving Sam standing on the steps holding the lasagna while other kids stared at him.

Dave, however, was feeling much better. And he couldn't have been happier. That very morning Dave had run into Mary Turlington.

Mary and Bert Turlington live two doors from Dave and Morley. Mary is an accountant, and she and Dave have rubbed each other the wrong way since the moment they met. It was something about Mary's politics, something about the way she dressed, the condescending way she talked about Dave's record store, that bugged Dave.

It was the way Dave seemed to glide through life without trying, that he didn't dress like a grown-up, that he made his living playing records, for heaven's sake— that was it, he played, he didn't work, that's what irked Mary.

"Dave," said Mary when they bumped into each other that Monday, "you look great."

"Really?" said Dave.

"Great," said Mary. "Fabulous."

It had been happening all weekend. Everyone he met had something nice to say. At first he had thought that it was no more than that. They were just being nice. But Mary Turlington was never nice to him. He *must* be looking good. There *was* something to Carl Lowbeer's herbal tonic after all.

At lunch Dave doubled his dose. When he walked back to work, there was a spring to his step. All afternoon he kept slipping in and out of the washroom, staring at his reflection in the mirror.

While Dave preoccupied himself with the mirror, Morley was on the phone dealing with George Daughtery.

George, who lives in the neighborhood, works for the telephone company. But George's brother-in-law runs a funeral parlor somewhere out of town. George's brother-in-law said that the best thing George could do for Morley and Dave was to help them make arrangements. In advance.

"People don't like talking about it," said George's brother-in-law, "but it's easier to face it sooner than later. They'll try to duck it. Don't let them."

George, who is so shy he has a hard time ordering in a restaurant, was vibrating with anxiety when he finally picked up the phone. He was so overwrought that it took him ten awkward minutes to get to the point.

"Oh," said Morley when she finally figured it out. "That's very sweet, George. That's very thoughtful. But a funeral just wouldn't be our style. I know some people do that sort of thing, but quite frankly I don't want to spend any more money on him."

"Perhaps," said George, screwing up all his courage, following his instructions, "you might consider cremation?"

"What?" said Morley. "And put him in an urn? George, it would be just one more damn thing to dust. We love him and everything, but when the time comes, we were thinking we would just put him in the backyard. It'll be good for the roses."

Morley put the phone down and smiled, thinking about how kind people could be. She sat at her desk, fiddling with a paper clip. All these neighbors concerned about a dog, about her family's problems. Just that morning Mary Turlington had brought over a sausage-and-onion lasagna. Morley was feeling reconnected, certainly feeling a lot better than George Daughtery, who had to report to his brother-in-law.

"That's ridiculous," said the brother-in-law. "Go see the husband."

George relunctantly set off to see Dave. He was carrying a seafood lasagna. He stopped along the way for a drink to fortify his courage.

"He says he doesn't need that sort of thing," he reported two hours later.

"Denial," said the brother-in-law. "Next stage is anger."

"He did get a little prickly," said George. "He asked me if I was on commission."

"Good," said the brother-in-law. "Acceptance is just a few stages away. Go back."

George wasn't cut out for this sort of thing. He went back to Dave's shop, but not with his heart and soul. He gave up almost as soon as he had begun his third pitch.

"I have to go," he said. "By the way, Dave, you're looking great."

"I know," said Dave.

That was the day that Stephanie phoned home from college and said, "Mom, the sweetest thing happened. I just got a card from the Lowbeers. It said, *Thinking of you in these difficult times*."

Stephanie was in the middle of exams.

It was also the worst day in Sam's life. Mrs. Estabrooks kept smiling at him. It was so obvious that everybody could see it. Kids were starting to lose patience. Even Murphy rolled his eyes. Sam was starting to feel guilty, his guilt heightened by his anxiety about Arthur. The vet was supposed to phone with word any day. And then on the way to music class Mrs. Estabrooks held him back.

"Sam," she said, "they want to see you in the office."

When he got to the office, Sam had to sit on the bench in the hall for fifteen minutes—in plain view. Everyone who walked by stared at him, as if he were in trouble. He thought, *It can't get worse than this*. Then it did.

A lady called Mrs. Gillespie took him from the bench and led him to the counseling room. Mrs. Gillespie was a counselor.

"I want you to tell me about your father," she said kindly.

Sam started to cry. He couldn't take it any longer.

"Not my father," he said. "My dog."

"Your what?" said Mrs. Gillespie.

"My dad isn't dying," said Sam. "My dog is."

"He's in bad shape," said Mrs. Gillespie to Mrs. Estabrooks forty-five minutes later. "He's in denial. He won't even admit his father is sick. He says it's the dog."

"What are you going to do?"

"I'll see him tomorrow. In the meantime, pay as much attention to him as you can."

At the end of the day, Mrs. Estabrooks made a point of giving Sam another pat on the back. Mark Portnoy was watching again. Sam couldn't stand it anymore. He had to set the record straight. He went home, planning to tell his mom. When he got there, his dad was already home. Dave was in the backyard with Morley. The barbecue was going, and the Turlingtons were leaning on the picnic table, chatting with his parents. Sam looked at his mom. She was laughing about something. He hadn't seen her so relaxed in months. His father was putting burgers on the barbecue. Mary Turlington had got up to help. And Arthur was there.

Arthur was home. He was bounding towards Sam, wagging his tail frenetically, his tongue lolling out of his mouth. Sam started to cry.

"Is he okay?" asked Sam.

"He is pretty okay for a fourteen-year-old dog," said Morley.

"Can I take him for a walk?" asked Sam. This wasn't the place where he had to set things right. Everything was already right here. He had to set things right at school.

He did that first thing the next morning.

"My dog is going to be all right," he said to Mrs. Estabrooks as soon as he saw her.

"Your dog or your dad?" said Mrs. Estabrooks.

"Yes," said Sam. "He isn't going to die after all. He's all better now. It wasn't so bad as we thought. They gave him pills."

"Really?" said Mrs. Estabrooks.

"Yeah," said Sam absently as he settled into his desk. "He just had worms."

Word spread through the neighborhood like wildfire.

PART IV

CIVIL

DISOBEDIENCE

TEETH

A story of illicit love, passion and the perils
of gardening; wherein Dave's dear and aged
neighbor, Eugene, succumbs to his appetites,
disobeys his wife and, we are led to believe,
may be called on to pay the ultimate price.

The relationship between a gardener and his or her
garden can be every bit as complicated as the relationship between two lovers.

Consider Eugene, for instance. Eugene lives next door
to Dave and Morley.

Consider the back corner of Eugene's garden, back by
the shed, the corner where every May, for the past fifty-two
years, Eugene has knelt down in the damp spring earth and
worked his fingers into the warm soil, grubbing out little
holes, each no deeper than two inches, each no wider than
a pencil stub. Into the holes, one by one, Eugene has carefully dropped his pocket full of leathery shrunken seeds—
each one holding within it the secret promise of September.
On his knees by the shed in May, dreaming of September,
Eugene plants his seeds prayerfully, still bewitched by the

wonder of God's earth, still enchanted by the seduction of sweet corn. This year, like last, Eugene planted Autumn Sunglow: a sweet, tender, variety of the famous Silver Queen.

As he covered each seed with a handful of dirt, then patted the soil down, Eugene imagined, like any lover might, the full ripeness of his beloved. The sweet ears of corn would be husked in the backyard where they grew, right where he was kneeling even now. Immediately they would be plunged into a bucket of ice-cold water. Eugene would carry the bucket into the kitchen. There he would drop each cob softly into water that was already set to boil, so the cobs could be cooked before any of the sugars knew what was happening to them, before they could even think of converting to starch. Once they were plucked from the hot water, the sweet cobs of corn would be laid gently on a plate—would, in no time at all, be swimming in butter, seasoned with salt. It would be seduction so perfect that just the thought of it would carry Eugene through the torpor of June, the fullness of July, the growing darkness of August.

All through the summer, Eugene watered and weeded, thinned and fertilized his corn like a lover caring for his true love, wishing and hoping and praying that his patience and his tenderness would eventually bestow the blessings of love upon him, that the garden he was tending would not break his heart.

But Eugene is not a young man, and although he has harvested corn every year for fifty-two years, and although he got down on his knees and planted it again this spring—his fifty-third summer in this garden—it has been many long autumns since he has sunk his teeth into a cob of sweet corn.

In fact, it has been many long years since he has sunk his teeth into anything.

The autumn he was seventy-five years old, Eugene and his wife, Maria, returned to Italy, to the province of Calabria, for two months. They went to the village of Rendi, to the thirty-acre farm where Eugene grew up—run now by his nephew, his late brother Tomasso's son.

"I have to see it. One last time," said Eugene to Maria all that summer. "It is my dying wish."

He never told Maria the real reason he wanted to go home, never told her that he couldn't stand another winter in Canada, with his teeth aching on every inhalation of cold winter air, with every cup of hot coffee.

He had tried to get his teeth fixed. He had gone to his dentist and said, "Pull them."

And his dentist, who every autumn imports a case of the small dark-leafed Tuscano-style cigars Eugene smokes and trades them for a trunkful of Eugene's homemade wine, wouldn't hear of it. "Don't be crazy," he said. "I won't do it. Never. Never."

So Eugene and Maria went to Calabria, and on their last afternoon there, Eugene went to Old Paolo, the dentist. When Eugene had left Rendi, Old Paolo had been Young Paolo. His father, the original Old Paolo, had passed the family business to his son, who had taken over the pliers and spittoon with energetic industry. Now, however, Young Paolo was Old Paolo, a startling echo of his father— stooped, half-blind and hairy.

When it was his turn in the chair, Eugene said to Old Paolo, "Out. All of them," and then sat there, his arms folded across his chest, his mouth wide open.

Eugene came home to Canada to get his false teeth. He thought it would be like going to the grocery. He thought a new crop of teeth would make him new with the world again. Eugene is a gardener; he believes in fresh starts.

No one warned Eugene that removing your teeth was like removing a limb. You can, if you work at it, manage without an arm or leg, but you have to *work* at it. You have to learn a whole new set of skills to get by.

All those years ago when he had got his new teeth, Eugene hadn't been interested in learning new skills. He put the teeth in his mouth and walked out of the dentist's office. He felt as if he were chewing on a hockey puck.

That was October the nineteenth, a week before his seventy-sixth birthday. Maria had invited half the neighborhood for dinner, including Bert and Mary Turlington, Carl and Gerta Lowbeer, Father Donkin and men from the Tivoli Club, where Eugene plays *scopa*. And, of course, Dave and Morley. Maria had spent the week getting ready. She had deep-fried squid and grilled potatoes and peppers in olive oil. There was fresh cheese, homemade wine, country bread from Bidaldo's with a crisp, hard crust and, naturally, a pot of sweet corn.

They had to put three tables together to hold everyone, making a table so long it stretched out of the kitchen and into the front hall. Eugene sat at the head of the long table in front of all these people, some of whom Maria barely knew. Eugene picked up the first cob, slathered it in butter, rolled it in salt and brought it up to his mouth. Everyone watched, smiling, waiting for him to begin—it was, after all, *his* birthday. Their eyes were still on him as Eugene bit into the corn with great gusto. The guests had not yet turned their attention to their own plates when Eugene pulled the cob back from his mouth. He drew the corn out of his mouth, and there was a tiny *pop,* and then the ear of corn was in the air above Eugene's dinner plate, wedged between his upper and lower teeth like a long yellow rat caught in a trap.

"Jesus and Mary," said Father Donkin.

It was the last bite of corn Eugene ever took. But he kept growing it. For years Eugene had grown his corn and given it away to his neighbors. But this year he wasn't going to live without it any longer. He had lived without it long enough.

Getting old, as Morley's mom, Helen, likes to say, is not a pastime for sissies. The frailties of old age are something Eugene has been ducking and denying for years—with astounding success. This is an especially impressive feat for a man who has smoked Parodis—those little Italian cigars—seemingly all day long all his life. But even Eugene knew his lucky streak was going to run out one day, and probably sooner rather than later. The thought of it made him grumpy. And so he had decided that he wasn't going another fall without a cob of his corn.

It finally finished ripening on a Tuesday in September. Eugene lay in bed that Tuesday night and was sure he could hear the corn, out of sight, by the shed, begging to be picked. Wednesday came like every Wednesday. Maria was up at five-thirty. She made her coffee and by six was sitting in the kitchen, her hair in curlers, getting ready for lunch club, reading the large-print edition of *Reader's Digest*.

By the time Eugene joined her at seven, Maria had moved on from *Reader's Digest* and was struggling with the newspaper, rereading for the fourth time a synopsis of the last season of a popular TV show. In the political drama, the president's daughter had just been kidnapped. Maria, who watched only soccer and ice-skating on TV, and who followed the news inconsistently, didn't realize she was reading about a television show. She thought the president's daughter had *actually* been kidnapped. It was a thought that terrified her. If the president's daughter could be kidnapped, no one was safe.

When Eugene shuffled into the kitchen, Maria looked up at her husband and said, "They still haven't found the president's daughter. It's been all summer."

Then she said, "Make sure you lock the door when I leave."

Eugene sat down heavily. Maria brought him his coffee and a bowl of fresh figs and melon.

Eugene stared at the bowl of fruit, reached into his dressing-gown pocket and pulled out his teeth. These days he mostly wears his teeth in his pocket, removing them from his pocket only when people come around or when it is time to eat.

Eugene had never liked the set of teeth his dentist had made him. In his darker moments he suspected that the dentist, who was horrified when Eugene had his teeth out, had made the teeth so they would torture him on purpose. But he never said anything about it. Eugene was worried if he said anything, he and the dentist might begin to feud. He could lose his annual supply of free cigars.

So instead of dealing with it up front, Eugene ordered sets of false teeth off the backs of health magazines and from the supermarket tabloids that Maria collects—stuffing his mouth with the soft plastic molds they sent him and returning them by mail.

He had a pair that made him whistle like a guinea pig, and another that clattered as if his mouth were full of marbles. Maria had outlawed both of these sets. But on this Wednesday afternoon, Maria was not going to be home. Eugene was free to use any set of teeth he felt like.

At noon, Eugene shuffled out to the end of the garden and picked two fat ripe ears of corn. He stuffed them into his pockets so his hands would be free as he made his way back to the kitchen.

The water was already boiling. There was a plate on the kitchen table. And salt. And butter. And lying beside them, the sturdiest set of false teeth Eugene owned—a pair of teeth that Eugene had bought at an antique store and had long forgotten, a pair that employed a stiff spring to keep them in place. The spring was armed to keep the teeth constantly open; it pushed against his lower and upper gums. The teeth were sitting on the table, wide open, looking like a leg-hold trap you might use on one of those vicious fur-bearing animals, like a wolverine.

Eugene lowered the two cobs of corn into the boiling water. He waited precisely three minutes and took them out. He carried them across the kitchen to the table and dropped them onto his plate. He sat down heavily, sighing with contentment as he did.

He picked up his teeth and brought them up to his mouth, opening wide as he tried to work them in.

They didn't fit.

In the open position, their default position, the teeth were too large to slide between his lips.

Eugene was puzzled. They used to work. Then he remembered that you had to force the spring closed and slip the teeth into your mouth in the closed position. When they were in place, you could release the pressure and the force of the spring would hold them in position.

Eugene picked up the teeth and, holding them in both hands as if he were holding a hamburger, he slipped them between his lips. Using his tongue to guide him, Eugene worked the teeth carefully back and forth, trying to get them to set down on his gums.

And when they did, Eugene had a moment—a second maybe, or maybe two—of pure pleasure as he sat at the kitchen table, looking down at his two ears of steaming corn. He was thinking to himself in that moment that life was grand, that even after all of these years, this old earth could feel fresh and new and pregnant with the promise of pleasure.

Eugene, with the pure joy of childhood, reached out and picked up the first ear of corn. He held it in front of him for a second.

He breathed in the rich smell of the melted butter. He sighed. It had been too long. He opened his mouth, and when he opened his mouth there was a faint click, like a car door unlocking, or a mousetrap going off in the night, or a spring beginning to unravel.

There was another click and another. Eugene put the corn back on the plate. The clicks, which seemed to be coming from inside him, had begun to repeat so fast they were now more of a whirring than a clicking. As Eugene sat there, trying not to move, his mouth began to open. He was not trying to open his mouth. His mouth was opening on its own—wider and wider.

Eugene's mouth was open wider than he would have believed possible. It was so wide that it felt as if he were going to swallow his own head. And then the teeth reached their maximum open position, and Eugene stood in the middle of his own kitchen, his mouth wide open, looking like a desperate baby bird waiting for a worm. *Now what do I do?* he thought.

The phone rang.

Eugene picked it up.

"UUH," he said.

"Eugene?" said Maria.

Thank God. It was his wife. Eugene tried to explain about the teeth.

"UH UH UUH UH UH," he said.

"Eugene. What is wrong?" said Maria, fear swelling in her voice.

"UH UH UH," said Eugene.

And then, amazingly, Maria understood: Eugene hadn't locked the door as she had told him. Her worst fears had come true. Kidnappers—probably the same ones who had the president's daughter—had her husband tied and gagged.

"Eugene," said Maria desperately, "I am coming home."

The thought of Maria rushing home and finding him wearing the forbidden teeth terrified Eugene.

He stuck a finger in his mouth and tried to lever the teeth out. He put one of his hands on top of his head and the other on his chin and he tried to push his mouth closed. He tried to do both things at the same time. For five minutes he stood in the kitchen and wrestled with his own head, in vain.

And then, realizing the futility, he stopped gasping for air and stared at the cobs of corn. After all these years, after all the close calls, all the near misses, is this how he was going to die? Ripped apart by a set of false teeth?

For giving in to the siren call of illicit love, for succumbing to passion (an emotion that belonged properly to the young, not to an old fool like him), for his weakness, Eugene was about to be handed the ultimate punishment.

He picked up his cane and lurched out the back door. He was heading for the place he always headed when something needed to be fixed. He was heading for his shed, knowing one thing: he had to get the teeth out before Maria got home.

He felt like a fool, but he wasn't going to let Maria find him this way. Not without a fight.

By the time he had stomped past his fig tree, Eugene had worked himself into a fury. His face, ruddy at the best of times, was bright red and dripping with sweat. He followed his wide-open mouth past his tomatoes, around the zucchinis, right through the melon patch. He looked like a snowblower.

He threw the shed door open and peered into the gloom. There had to be something in the shed he could use to lever the teeth closed.

It took Eugene fifteen minutes to wrestle the wine press out of the shed and into the garden. Five minutes to pad it up with a couple of old towels and crank it open.

By the time Sam and his friend Murphy yawped down the alley like a pair of crows, Eugene had his head in the wine press and had the press screwed down as tight as he could get it. He was so mad, so worked up, so furious at what he had done to himself that his face was now more purple than red.

Sam and Murphy almost walked right by him.

"UH UH," said Eugene.

Sam and Murphy stopped in their tracks.

The sight of the old man with his head in the wine press was so beyond anything the boys had ever seen that they had difficulty making sense of what they were looking at. Sam didn't recognize Eugene—he just saw component parts, as if he were looking at a painting by Picasso. There was a worn blue suit jacket with gray stripes, a red face, a brown shoe jerking up and down, a head of gray hair in disarray.

It was different for Murphy. For Murphy, it was as if he were looking through a tunnel. Everything faded away except for the purple head in the wine press. The head, ruddier than any face he had ever seen, was held in some sort of murderous medieval torture device, just like the ones he had read about in *Ripley's Believe It or Not*.

Murphy was beginning to feel queasy.

"UH UH UH," said Eugene, gesturing wildly.

And that's when the sneeze began.

It began as a tickle at the front of Eugene's nose, right at the tip, and then spread back into him like electricity. It was building inside of him—in that spot where his nasal cavity and his throat and his lungs all join like some seldom-visited railway yard.

Eugene decided at the last moment, as the air rushed down his nose, that it would be better, with the boys standing there, to divert the sneeze from his nose to his mouth. He did this in an instant, like a railroad controller flicking a switch and sending a runaway train off the main line and onto a side rail. The sneeze, however, was building force, so it rushed through his mouth like a tropical storm—like a hurricane blowing over a shingled roof—driving his teeth out of his mouth and sending them flying across the backyard.

When Murphy was in grade one, some kid in the schoolyard had told him that a sneeze could build up in a person with such force that it could blow their head apart. Murphy had worried about this ever since, had been seized with the cold grip of death every time he felt a sneeze coming on. He would squeeze his eyes shut as each sneeze raced out his nose, not wanting to see his own brain exploding in front of his face.

So when this man with the monstrously purple face had the sneeze squeezed out of him, Murphy covered his eyes with his hands.

Sam's eyes, however, opened wider. Eugene sneezed and suddenly the picture came into focus for Sam: Sam saw everything with the clarity that athletes sometimes describe when they speak of heightened moments of awareness. Eugene sneezed, and Sam saw the teeth fly out Eugene's mouth, coming toward him like some sort of vicious grin. Acting on instinct alone, Sam reached out and plucked the teeth out of the air—the second greatest catch of his life.

There was dead silence.

Then Murphy peered through his fingers and saw Sam holding the old man's teeth. It was just as they had told him in the schoolyard—the old man had blown his head apart.

Murphy vomited.

Two months will pass before Sam and Eugene have their next dental rendezvous.

In those two months, Sam will learn he has to have braces on his teeth. The very same afternoon that Sam gets this bad news, Eugene will spot him over the fence and he will notice Sam has been crying.

Eugene will wave him over and Sam, who will have thought he was alone with his misery, will wipe his nose on his sleeve, go over to Eugene's backyard and sit down on one of the old kitchen chairs Eugene keeps there—the chair Eugene sits on to watch things grow.

When Sam tells Eugene that the braces are going to ruin his life, Eugene will nod sympathetically.

"You're right," he will say. "They could do that."

And he will reach into his pocket and pull out his little red-and-white package of miniature cigars and offer one to Sam.

"I don't smoke," Sam will say.

Eugene will shrug. "I forgot," he will say. And then he will hold the package out again and say, "It's never too soon to start."

Eugene will work his teeth loose with his tongue and slip them out and pocket them. Sam will say, "Maybe I should have my teeth pulled. Then I wouldn't need braces."

Eugene will get up and take him into the shed and reach among the orange clay flowerpots on one of the shelves and pull out a bottle of his homemade wine. "I guess you still don't drink either?" he'll ask. Sam will shake his head.

"Too bad," Eugene will say.

And they will go back to the chairs and sit there for a half an hour, the old man and the boy, and by the time Sam has to go, they will have talked about many things.

And one afternoon the next September, the two of them will sit down again, this time in Eugene's kitchen. Even though Sam will be wearing braces, and even though corn, like gum and toffee, will be on his list of forbidden foods, Sam and Eugene will eat fresh corn together: Sam with his shiny new braces and a juice glass full of toothpicks beside him, Eugene using his penknife to cut the kernels off his cob.

Eugene will sit there with butter dribbling down his chin, and smile. "You should never, never never give up on something you love," he will say.

Then he will put his fork down and pick up his glass of wine. He will look out his window at his garden, he will hold his glass up to the corn and the pepper plants and his fig tree and the beans still on the vine, and he will turn to the boy, lean forward and smile.

"It's not," he will say, "what happens to you that matters. It's what you *think* about what happens to you. That's what counts."

DAVE AND THE DENTIST

An inconsequential story of little merit that contains gratuitous descriptions of shocking behavior that some readers are bound to find disturbing and that should be skipped by anyone who has ever written letters of complaint to newspapers, publishers and especially authors.

It was inevitable that the chocolates should have come from Mary Turlington.

"She said they had soft centers," said Dave.

"I don't remember that," said Morley. "I don't remember her saying *anything* about the chocolates, except that they were her favorites."

"Her favorite *creams*," said Dave. "She said *creams*."

"I don't remember that," said Morley. "Are you trying to say this is *her* fault?"

Then Morley leaned towards Dave and whispered, "Do you think it's ... a plot?"

It was a Sunday afternoon. One of those sunny Sundays when you suddenly believe that you might make it to the end of winter after all. The sky was bright blue. The world was light.

Dave was lying on the couch. He was clutching a hot-water bottle. It wasn't sunny or light by the couch. By the couch, it was gloomy and heavy. It was *raining* by the couch.

Dave dropped the hot-water bottle on the floor and said, "This isn't helping."

Morley shrugged and kept reading. Morley was reading the paper.

"There's a guy here who says Lady Bird Johnson was on the grassy knoll," said Morley a few minutes later.

Dave wasn't listening. "Soft centerd," he grumbled. "She said that. Absolutely."

Dave was talking about a box of chocolates, some dark and glistening, others soft and milky. Chocolates wrapped in shiny green and gold foil. Actually, he was talking about one particular chocolate—an almond toffee crunch.

Mary Turlington had brought the chocolates when she and Bert had come for dinner the night before.

"She *said* they were creams."

"Imagine," said Morley, sighing as she folded the paper and headed for the kitchen. "Lady Bird Johnson. It makes so much sense. But who would have guessed?"

"You're only pretending not to hear me," said Dave. "That was a theatrical sigh." Then he said, "Where you going?"

Morley didn't answer. Morley wasn't going—Morley was gone.

Okay, so he bit into the chocolate harder than he should have. Certainly harder than he would have if he had known it was an almond toffee crunch. He didn't actually *feel* his tooth break. You'd think there would be pain if you cracked a piece off one of your teeth, but there was no pain. In fact, there was no sensation whatsoever. Suddenly, there was just something in his mouth that wasn't chocolate and wasn't toffee. Dave was sitting at the dinner table with the Turlingtons when this happened. To his credit, he *tried* to be discreet. He slipped the piece of something into his hand, and from there into his pocket, so he could examine it later. He sent his tongue, not his fingers, darting around his mouth to check for damage. His tongue landed on a tooth at the back of his mouth. Or, more accurately, it landed where there *used* to be a tooth and where there was tooth no more.

Maybe five minutes passed. For five minutes, Dave sat at the dinner table, smiling vacantly at the conversation around him while he explored this strange new place with his tongue. It was a disturbing turn of events but not an overwhelming one—until the idea of infection awoke in him. Hadn't he read something about dental health and heart disease? Hadn't he read something about people taking antibiotics before they went to the dentist? As if it had a mind of its own, his tongue continued to flick around the space left by the broken tooth. It was impossible to tell how deep the hole was. For all Dave knew, things were being sucked up through this hole directly into his brain. That couldn't be good.

Someone was calling his name. It was Morley.

"Dave?" said Morley.

"Oh."

Everyone at the table was looking at him. And they all seemed to be expecting something. Dave smiled and reached for his water. He was stalling, trying to gather it up, trying to reconstruct the conversation that had been going on around him.

Had he been thinking straight, Dave would have put the water down without taking a sip. But he wasn't thinking straight. So instead, still stalling, he brought the glass to his mouth. When the ice water hit the exposed tooth, it felt as if someone had driven an ice pick into his brain. For the briefest instant, his brain was the only thing that reacted. *Mistake,* thought his brain. Then the mouthful of water, mixed with what remained of the almond toffee chocolate, fire-hosed out of his mouth, arced across the table and hit Mary Turlington just above her décolletage.

That had been Saturday night. Now it was Sunday afternoon. There was still a good eighteen hours before Dave could call the dentist—something he hadn't done for almost ten years.

Dr. Peter O'Hagan probably shouldn't have gone into dentistry in the first place. Dr. O'Hagan has a bit of the Irish in him—a deep melancholic vein that would have best been left undisturbed and that might have remained so if he had chosen a less stressful profession, a profession like, say, auto mechanics. Auto mechanics is not altogether dissimilar work from dentistry. You open something, and you fiddle around. But they are fundamentally different all the same; a car engine, unlike a mouth containing teeth, cannot express a thought. And every day, when he headed to work, Dr. O'Hagan knew someone was going to have something to say that would upset him.

Sometimes it would be the very first patient, and that would be it for the rest of the day. Dr. O'Hagan would spend the entire night psyching himself up, convincing himself that dentistry was his calling, that he was doing good, necessary work. And he would head to work full of hope and smile at the first person who came through the door. Let's call that first patient Bob.

"Bob," Dr. O'Hagan would say, "how are you?"

Bob would drop into the chair, glare at Dr. O'Hagan and say something like, "I was fine until I got *here*." And Dr. O'Hagan would shrink a little inside.

It wore him down. That sort of thing, week in, week out, would wear anyone down. But Dr. O'Hagan kept grinding along, surrounded by patients who seemed to think that excavating tooth decay and watching people spit into a sink was something you could enjoy. At least once a week someone muttered, "I can't believe I'm *paying* you to make my gums bleed."

There were all sorts of whiners and flinchers. Like Mrs. Slavin, who carried a bottle of eucalyptus to sniff while Dr. O'Hagan was working on her. She said it helped her gag reflex. It didn't. Or Leora Moore, who would begin to moan before he touched her. Dr. O'Hagan only had to walk into the room and Leora Moore would start moaning, even if she was there only for a checkup.

And there was Dave.

Dave is not his best self in the dentist's office. He has a history with the profession that began when he was a boy.

Now, if the world were a perfect place, Dr. O'Hagan and Dave would never have crossed paths. If the world were a perfect place, Dr. O'Hagan would have only patients who were obsessive-compulsives and showed up cheerfully for their weekly cleaning and polishing.

But the world is not a perfect place. It is fate's cruel way that Dave and Dr. O'Hagan were brought together.

Dr. O'Hagan brought his melancholic streak to the union. Dave brought fear.

Fear was sewn into Dave's soul, when he was a child, by the only other dentist Dave has known—the infamous Dr. Rejean Thom.

Dr. Thom was the only dentist in the town of Big Narrows, where Dave grew up. And Dr. Thom was a bully.

Dr. Thom would hover over Dave as if he were about to reach into a cadaver, his big meaty fingers wiggling back and forth. "Open your mouth wider, boy," he would grunt. And while Dave sat in the chair like a fledging waiting for a worm, Dr. Thom would bark, "Wider!"

It was Dr. Thom who told Dave he had soft teeth. He made it sound like an accusation, as if soft teeth were a sign of moral weakness.

It was Dr. Thom who waved pliers in Dave's face and said, "If you don't do a better job brushing your teeth, I'm going have to yank them out."

It was Dr. Thom who didn't believe in anesthetic.

Dave still has dreams of Dr. Thom peering down at him gleefully, his drill wiggling back and forth. In those dreams Dr. Thom is always saying the same thing, the thing he always said when he hurt Dave: "That didn't hurt, now, did it?"

It was Dr. Thom who laid the battleground between Dave and the melancholic Peter O'Hagan.

"It's not fair," said Dave to Morley after one disastrous appointment. "He had all those sharp instruments. All I had were my teeth."

That appointment had begun almost hopefully. Dr. O'Hagan had fitted Dave with his new audio headsets. Dave lay back and cranked up Creedence Clearwater Revival as high as he could crank them. He was· so absorbed with the novelty of the headsets that he forgot he was at the dentist. The music was humming in his ears.

The light from the dentist's overhead lamp was warming his face. He stretched out on the leatherette recliner and closed his eyes. He felt as if he were lying on a beach chair. He began to drift off.

Pretty soon the beach chair had become a chaise longue. Pretty soon he was lying on a chaise longue, on a dock, by a sparkling lake. The radio was playing beside him; the summer sun was beating on his face. He was thinking about reaching for a cold bottle of beer when someone suddenly leapt from behind his chair and shoved a beach towel into his open mouth. That's when Dave woke up.

Actually, and sadly, that's not true. Dave didn't wake up. What happened was Dave *thought* he had woken up, but he was only dreaming that he had woken up. In his dream he was sitting in a dentist's chair and the nefarious Dr. Thom was standing above him, shoving a beach towel down his throat. The crazed dentist was wearing a goalie mask, like the guy in that horror movie, and he had one hand in Dave's mouth and was reaching for a second beach towel. It was when Dave heard Dr. Thom's dental hygienist, who was standing beside the doctor, saying, "Let's get the beach umbrella in there too" that he knew he had to take action.

If he had woken, he might still have bitten Dr. O'Hagan, but it would have been one of those short, involuntary bites that dentists are accustomed to. He would have closed his teeth, and then opened them the instant

Dr. O'Hagan started screaming. He wouldn't have clamped down on Dr. O'Hagan's finger the way he did, shaking his head back and forth like a dog.

You would have thought Dr. O'Hagan's scream would have woken Dave. But Dave had the headsets on, and so loud. So he didn't wake up, didn't see the nurse running to Dr. O'Hagan's side or hear the patients fleeing from the waiting room.

That was the last time Dave went to Dr. O'Hagan. That was ten years ago. But now he needed a dentist, and he didn't know anyone else. So, Monday evening, when Dave arrived at Dr. O'Hagan's office with his broken tooth, both of them were anxious.

Dr. O'Hagan was surprised to see Dave's name on the appointment list. Ten years is a long time between appointments. He had assumed he was never going to see Dave again.

"Where did he get our new address?" he asked his secretary peevishly. When Dr. O'Hagan had moved his office, he had quietly pulled Dave's notification from the pile in his secretary's outbox and thrown it away.

The day had not been going well. Modern dental equipment is designed to work on people who are lying down. There are, however, people who don't like to do that, who refuse to have their seat put back. Dr. O'Hagan had one of those people first thing that Monday morning, and that meant that to do the work that had to be done, he had

had to twist and turn as if he were working in the Cirque du Soleil. By lunchtime, Dr. O'Hagan's back was aching and he was behind schedule. He had to skip lunch. By the time Dave dropped reluctantly into Dr. O'Hagan's chair at 5:45, Dr. O'Hagan was starving and cranky.

Dave was already lying on the chair when Dr. O'Hagan came into the room. They had both decided, independently, that it would be best if they didn't mention their last appointment. Neither of them did.

"I have broken a tooth," said Dave, pointing with his forefinger.

His finger was covering at least four teeth.

Dr. O'Hagan picked up a prod.

"You aren't going to touch it?" said Dave, pulling back. "It's the one that hurts."

Dr. O'Hagan arched his back and took a deep breath.

A short time later Dave's mouth was frozen and Dr. O'Hagan was working on the broken tooth with his drill. He was cleaning up the decay so he could patch it. When the drill was running, Dr. O'Hagan could ignore Dave's flinching and thrashing about, but each time he stopped, Dave would begin mumbling. His mouth was full of cotton wads, making his speech incoherent, but to Dr. O'Hagan, Dave sounded vaguely threatening.

"Mahwee Churwinchon, dam Mahwee Churwinchon," was all Dr. O'Hagan could make out. It was making him nervous.

Dave and Dr. O'Hagan were half an hour into their ordeal when things took a dramatic turn. One moment Dr. O'Hagan was pressing the drill into a soft patch in Dave's tooth. The next moment Dave's tooth was falling to pieces, right in front of Dr. O'Hagan's eyes. Dr. O'Hagan gasped.

Dave heard the gasp and gripped the armrests harder, but he didn't open his eyes.

Dr. O'Hagan could feel the muscles tensing around his neck and shoulders. He still had a pleasant smile plastered on his face. How do you tell a patient that the tooth you were working on just self-destructed? How do you tell them that you've just made their tooth worse instead of better?

"Uh," said Dr. O'Hagan. "This might take a little longer than I had thought. There's not much tooth to work with anymore."

Dr. O'Hagan's back was throbbing. Dr. O'Hagan was faint with hunger. Dr. O'Hagan needed to pee. This was not going the way Dr. O'Hagan wanted it to go.

Dave was now clutching the chair tightly enough to leave an imprint of his fingernails in the imitation leather. He seemed to be whimpering.

Dr. O'Hagan said, "Let's put a little more freezing in."

He had already put in two carpules. Dr. O'Hagan reached for a third. One in 100,000: not the most powerful dosage, but more than normal. He was going to do a nerve block. It would freeze a quarter of Dave's face and half of his tongue.

Dr. O'Hagan began to drill. Dr. O'Hagan said, "You might feel a little pinch."

Dave winced. Dave said, "I felt more than a pinch."

Dr. O'Hagan wiped the sweat from his brow and said, "Maybe you would like a bit more freezing."

"I want it," slurred Dave, nodding his head up and down vigorously. "Keep it coming."

Dr. O'Hagan was fighting for his life. He had started this thing and it had gone wrong, but there was no stopping now. They had to finish.

Dr. O'Hagan looked at Dave and tried to judge whether, in fact, Dave could take more Xylocaine.

He drew up a needle. And then he thought, *What the hell.*

He bent over, stretched his arm behind him and plunged it into his own aching back. Then he drew another and gave it to Dave.

And soon enough, it was over.

"It's over," said Dr. O'Hagan. "We're finished."

He sprayed Dave's mouth with mouthwash—wintergreen flavor.

Dave felt a wave of release wash over him. He brought his hand up to his face. His tongue felt like a pillow. He pulled himself unsteadily out of the dentist's chair.

"Are you okay?" asked Dr. O'Hagan.

Dave said, "I am goin' home an have a shringk."

"Me too," said Dr. O'Hagan.

Xylocaine works by changing the electrolyte balance of a nerve. You change the electrolyte balance, and that changes the nerve's capability to transmit pain.

When Dave left Dr. O'Hagan's office, he had enough Xylocaine in him to immobilize a small horse. Dave was exhausted, but he was feeling no pain.

Dave was stopped by the RIDE program half a mile from Dr. O'Hagan's office. He had done nothing wrong, but he felt guilt settle on him as he pulled over to the curb. It was the same guilt that settled on him whenever he was confronted by anyone in a uniform: customs officials, immigration functionaries, theatre ushers.

He rolled down his window and smiled at the officer shining the flashlight in his face. At least, he *thought* he was smiling. It was difficult to tell, as he seemed to have lost all control over his facial muscles.

He was drooling.

"Gud evenick, offissshur," he said.

The policeman leaned forward and tried to smell Dave's breath. Wintergreen. *Oldest trick in the book,* thought the cop.

"Had anything to drink tonight, sir?" said the officer, leaning even closer.

Dave had to concentrate to speak clearly. "I haven hud a shing to shringk," he said.

The policeman nodded pleasantly and said, "Could you wait here a moment, sir?" And he walked away.

He came back with another officer. The second officer asked Dave to step out of the car. Then he asked Dave to walk a straight line, one foot in front of the other.

Dave walked in a straight line.

More or less.

He asked Dave to touch his nose.

Dave attempted to look calm and cooperative. He reached up to his face. He couldn't find his nose. His nose seemed to have disappeared. Dave frowned and felt around his face. He looked at the cop and grinned nervously.

He said, "My fashe is compreewy numb."

His finger landed on his cheek about an inch west of his nose.

"Hewe?" he asked uncertainly.

As Dave tried to locate his nose, the first officer brought a small machine out of the cruiser. He asked Dave to blow.

His levels were fine.

"Well, it's not alcohol," said the first cop to the second, "but this guy is clearly higher than a kite."

They put Dave in the back of the car. They said, "We don't think you should be driving, sir."

And that was when Dr. O'Hagan drove by. He was so spent by his appointment with Dave that he hadn't even helped his hygienist tidy the equipment before he'd bolted from the office. He wasn't more than a few blocks from his building when he saw the flashing police lights and spotted Dave standing beside the cruiser, his arm outstretched, slowly moving his extended finger past his nose and into his own eye. Dr. O'Hagan pulled off the road, a block from the police car, and watched in his rearview mirror as an officer hustled Dave into the cruiser and drove away.

Dr. O'Hagan smiled as the police car drove by him.

"Bye, bye," said Dr. O'Hagan under his breath.

Maybe there was justice in this world after all. Maybe they would lock up Dave the biter forever. Dave had made an appointment for a six-month checkup as he had left. Maybe he would miss it.

Those thoughts lasted about five seconds.

It wasn't Dave's fault, after all. It wasn't Dave who had, all those years ago, filled out the application to dental college. Dave wasn't with Dr. O'Hagan when he stood in the college guidance office and put back the pamphlet on art history and picked up the one on dentistry instead. Dr. O'Hagan was a dentist. It was his profession and his livelihood.

He knew a lot of his patients didn't look forward to their appointments, but he also knew that along with the apprehension, the reluctance and even the grumpiness, his patients also felt relief, and even gratitude.

Dr. O'Hagan remembered that when Dave stumbled out of the dental chair half an hour ago, he had immediately stuck his finger in his mouth and moved it over the smooth rebuilt tooth. His brow had softened, and he had mumbled a rather pathetic "thank you" before lurching out the door.

There was no getting around it—Dr. O'Hagan had many days yet to spend with the Daves and Leoras and Mrs. Slavins of the world. But as long as there were a few "thank yous" peppering those days, he could, just like his patients, get through the worst of it.

Dr. O'Hagan turned on the car stereo. Vivaldi's *Four Seasons* was playing. "Spring." He reclined his car seat, closed his eyes and listened to the music. When the final strains of the allegro sounded, he sat back up. He was humming contentedly as he pulled into the police station parking lot, about to explain to the officers inside about the wonders of Xylocaine.

THE LAUNDRY CHUTE

A history of the heart, and of other things
that make hearts beat (not least of them, the
transgression of household rules); contains
matters both profound and sentimental,
and some trivial matters too.

Spring comes to the Cape Breton highlands later than it
does to other parts of this country. It comes even later to
Dave's hometown, the village of Big Narrows. When it
comes, it comes on the sudden cry of a crow flapping
over the hill behind the Macaulays' farm. The sound of
the crow came on a Wednesday last year, and it brought
Old Man Macaulay sprinting out of the barn. He stood in
his muddy farmyard squinting into the pale sun, as sure
a sign of spring as any crow, his dog beside him, tail
wagging, head cocked, staring into the sky too.

Overnight the snow on all the hills turned granular, and
little rivers began appearing everywhere. All the kids in
town got wet, and pretty soon everything smelled of damp
wool.

By the weekend, even the adults had joined in the festivities. On Saturday afternoon, it seemed everyone in the Narrows was out in their yard trying to hurry spring along—chipping away at stubborn piles of snow with shovels, hoes and axes.

On Sunday, Dave's mother, Margaret, went to work on the snow along the north side of her garage. When she had had enough, Margaret made a sandwich and sat in the backyard with her shirtsleeves rolled up, the sun warming her skin for the first time in months. That night she sat in the parlor and listened to *Turandot*—Puccini's great operatic testament to love. She listened to the old vinyl albums her late husband, Charlie, had given her. "Why would I want a CD player?" she had said. "Is the music any different on CDs?"

"Exactly," said her son, Dave.

On Monday, Margaret, struck with the promise of spring, decided it was warm enough to walk downtown to get the mail.

She stopped at MacDonnell's Grocery and picked up a pint of milk for her tea. And that was when the most unexpected thing in the world happened. In a few days, Margaret's friend Rose will call from Dayton, Ohio, and Margaret will tell her the whole story, in minute detail, except for the moment when it all began—the moment in MacDonnell's Grocery. That part is a blank, like the moments before an accident.

Margaret was chatting with Julie Doucette about something, for the life of her she can't remember what. Margaret and Julie were chatting about *something*— maybe the weather, maybe how nice it was to be warm again—when Margaret noticed the display table by the door. There was a sign taped to the table: *Big Narrows Volunteer Fire Department: Home Safety Inspections.*

It wasn't, however, the sign that caught Margaret's attention. It was the man sitting behind the table.

"He was adorable," said Margaret when she was telling the story to Rose.

He was the most adorable man Margaret had seen for years. He was wearing a soft plaid shirt—cotton—and a beige Windbreaker. He had thin gray hair and large ears, and before Margaret knew what she was doing, she was talking to him.

His name was Smith Gardner. A widower, it turned out. He told Margaret he was new in town—used to be the fire chief in Port Hawkesbury. He had moved to the Narrows because his daughter and his grandchildren were there. Margaret, a dozen years widowed, signed up for a home inspection.

"I'll put you down for Thursday morning," said the adorable man.

Margaret went right home and started cleaning. *Deep* cleaning. She dragged the scatter rugs into the backyard, slung them over the clothesline and beat them to within an inch of their lives. She mopped *and* waxed the kitchen floor. She vacuumed everything—even the drapes. She polished the silver. She attacked the linen closet and the upstairs bedrooms.

On Thursday morning, she was waiting in her kitchen when Angus McLeod pulled into her front yard in his red pickup and walked up to her front door carrying a clipboard.

"Hello, Margaret," said Angus. "They sent me over to do a safety inspection."

Margaret had been expecting the adorable man in the soft plaid shirt. She stared at Angus as if he had arrived from outer space. As if he didn't live two streets over.

"Angus McLeod," she heard herself say, "you are not inspecting *my* house. I want someone with a little more experience than you."

And then Margaret, who is known throughout the Narrows as one of the kindest and most sensitive women in the village, shut the door in Angus McLeod's face.

"Oh my," she said, her back to the door, her hand at her mouth.

She watched Angus through the kitchen curtains as he drove away.

Leonard Milton showed up two hours later. Margaret sent Leonard away too.

"Leonard Milton," she said, "not you."

On Friday afternoon, Arnie Gallagher called. Arnie the florist, the funeral-home director, the gift-store manager and the travel agent. Arnie the fire chief and the mayor.

"Margaret," said Arnie, "is everything okay?"

"Everything is fine, Arnie," said Margaret.

"People have been saying that you are not yourself."

"People talk foolishness," said Margaret.

"People are worried," said Arnie.

"They shouldn't worry," said Margaret.

Arnie said, "Okay then," and hung up.

He phoned back an hour later.

"Margaret," said Arnie, "I have been thinking on things. I have been thinking that I have been sending you men who aren't as experienced as you might require. Margaret, there is a new gentleman in town. He used to be chief of the Port Hawkesbury Fire Department. I think he might have the sort of experience necessary to inspect a house like yours."

Margaret said, "That would be just fine, Arnie."

Smith Gardner arrived at Margaret's house the following Tuesday, just after lunch. He was wearing a gray fisherman's sweater with a rolled neck. He said, "I'll start upstairs and work my way down." He smelled of Old Spice. Dave's father—Margaret's late husband, Charlie—was an Old Spice man.

The inspection took Smith twenty minutes. When he was finished, he walked into the kitchen.

"You need a smoke detector upstairs," he said. "The cord on the big lamp in the living room should be replaced. Otherwise you're in good shape. I'll write it up."

He didn't seem to be in a hurry to leave.

"Would you like a muffin?" said Margaret.

Smith sat down. He nodded at the baseball cap hanging by the back door. "Yankee fan?" he asked.

Margaret told him all about her trip to New York City.

"Charlie and I had always planned on going together," she said.

She told him about how she had gone by herself. How she had met Rose in the lobby of the Chelsea Hotel.

"Rose bought me the hat," she said. "I wear it in the garden." She was warming her hands on her mug of tea.

"Going to New York," she said, "meeting Rose, changed my life."

They sat silently for a few moments and then she said, "When your wife died ... did people stop including you?"

Smith Gardner smiled and nodded slightly.

Then Margaret said, "My friends would only have me over on the nights their husbands went out. I was okay for girls' nights, but not for the nights people really got together."

"Like you would upset the balance," said Smith.

He stayed for two hours. Margaret told him about her grandchildren—Sam and Stephanie in Toronto, Margot in Halifax.

Smith had just finished telling Margaret about *his* grandchildren when she picked up a towel and wiped at the table absentmindedly. She stood and walked across the kitchen and opened a tiny door in the wainscotting of the kitchen wall. She threw the towel in and shut the door.

"Whoa," said Smith, rising out of his chair. "Is that a laundry chute?"

He was so alarmed, it scared Margaret.

"I'm sorry," he said. "It's a huge fire hazard. If you would like I could come back and seal it up."

He said he could fix the lamp cord too. And bring a smoke detector.

Margaret said, "That would be nice."

He said, "I better be going, then." But he didn't leave for another hour.

After he left Margaret picked up her New York Yankees baseball cap and fiddled with it. She put it on. She went into the bathroom and stared at her reflection in the mirror. She twirled the hat around so the peak was facing backwards.

"Play ball," said Margaret.

Then she phoned Rose.

"It sounds like you are falling in love," said Rose.

"Don't be ridiculous," said Margaret. "I'm too old to fall in love."

"How old are you?" said Rose, who had been dying to ask.

"There's an eight in it," said Margaret.

That afternoon Margaret wandered around her house aimlessly—walked between the parlor and the living room in a daze until she came to with her hand on the laundry-chute door, not at all sure how long she had been standing there.

She was thinking of the night the barn swallow got trapped in the chute—remembering how she and Charlie had tried everything to get the bird out. Eventually, Charlie had dropped one of Annie's toy umbrellas down the chute from the top floor. The tiny open umbrella floated down slowly, like in a René Magritte painting. The bird flew out into the basement. It took them another hour to wave it out a basement window.

Then she remembered the time Charlie left his painting tray at the base of the chute, and Annie's favorite plaid skirt landed in the paint.

And how Dave used to toss Annie's stuffed animals down it.

Margaret got a flashlight from under the kitchen sink. The batteries were dead. She ransacked the house, but she couldn't find batteries anywhere. She drove to MacDonnell's and bought some. When she got home, she peered up the chute with the flashlight. If Smith Gardner was going to board the chute up, she wanted to see the little piece of leather hanging up there one last time.

The scrap of leather got there in 1959, the year after the last big bump at Springhill. Dave was still a young boy, Annie even younger.

Margaret had gone out to take food up to her sister, who had lost her Donny when the mine went down.

She felt guilty about what had happened after she left her house, but it wasn't as if she hadn't told David a hundred times that the laundry chute wasn't a toy.

"It's not a toy, and it's not a slide."

"Don't drop your trucks down the chute, David. Don't drop anything down that chute except your clothes. Your *dirty* clothes. And for heaven's sake, don't lean into it like that."

What could she do? She couldn't be home all the time. Margaret was taking a roast chicken to her poor lost sister.

And Dave, nine years old, alone at home with *his* little sister, was playing "Springhill mining disaster."

They began to mine for coal in Springhill, Nova Scotia, in the 1800s. By 1958, the coal mine in Springhill was one of the deepest mines in the world. The number-two colliery—the colliery that collapsed—was a labyrinth of tunnels and caverns. At the face of the mine it was more than fourteen thousand feet deep.

It was a couple of hours after supper on a Thursday evening near the end of October when the mine face collapsed. People who lived in Springhill knew what had happened right away. It was like an earthquake when it went. Phones bounced off tables. Pictures fell off walls. Off-duty coal men dropped what they were doing and ran to the mine.

One hundred seventy-four men were trapped under-ground.

By dawn they had seventy-five of them on the surface. That's when the real work began. Soon men were heading for Springhill from all over Nova Scotia to help. Dave's dad, Charlie, drove five miners from Glace Bay.

It was one of the biggest disasters in North American mining history, and the first disaster to be broadcast live on television. The story went all over the States. But there were no TVs to watch in the Narrows. Dave listened on the radio.

On the next Thursday, a week after the collapse, they brought twelve miners up alive.

On Friday, with men still missing, Prince Philip, the Duke of Edinburgh, who had been in Ottawa, visited the site with Premier Stanfield.

They brought the last living men up on Sunday.

Seventy-five men didn't make it—including Dave's uncle Donny.

A group of the rescued miners went to New York City and appeared on the *Ed Sullivan Show*. Another group was offered a free vacation on Jekyll Island by Marvin Griffin, the segregationist governor of Georgia. It was a publicity stunt that didn't turn out the way Governor Griffin had hoped—there was a miner from Africville in the group.

It was on a night about a year after the bump that Margaret said, "I am taking this roast chicken up to your aunt Elizabeth."

It was about twenty minutes after she left that Dave called Annie.

"I need your help," he said earnestly. "I am pretending this is a mine shaft. I have to climb to the bottom of the shaft."

"You can't do that," said Annie. "You aren't allowed."

"I have to," said Dave.

"Why do you have to?" asked Annie.

"There are men trapped down there," said Dave.

Annie frowned. She was only five years old. She wasn't tall enough to see into the chute, but she was pretty sure there weren't men down there.

"I don't hear them," she said.

Dave went into her bedroom and came back with an armful of stuffed animals. He threw the animals into the laundry chute.

"There," he said.

Dave was wearing a Windbreaker and a toque. He had a flashlight stuck in his belt. He pushed a chair under the laundry-chute door.

"You aren't allowed," said Annie.

Dave looked at his little sister earnestly. "Look," he said. "Mom doesn't know everything. We do lots of things we aren't supposed to do. We aren't supposed to stand up on toboggans, and we aren't supposed to ride cows. We aren't supposed to play in the creek with our clothes on."

"I don't do any of that stuff," said Annie.

"We aren't supposed to go outside in the winter with wet hair," said Dave. "You do that."

"That's because I like the way it freezes," said Annie.

"You aren't supposed to do it," said Dave. "I have to rescue the men at the bottom of this shaft," said Dave. "I need you to hold the rope."

Dave handed his sister the end of the rope that was tied around his waist. He climbed onto the chair and then pushed his leg through the chute opening. Then, holding on to the sides of the chute, he hoisted his other leg through the hole. He began to lower himself into the laundry chute, bracing himself by pushing his feet and his arms into the wall in front of him and his back into the wall behind. It was harder than he had imagined. He had wormed his way about eight feet down before he realized he wasn't going to be strong enough to make it all the way to the bottom.

There and then, doubt seized him, and then, as doubt always does to the weary, it overtook him, and Dave felt a rush of fear. He called his sister's name.

"Annie," he called.

Before she could answer, Dave was dropping down the chute like a stone. The rope burned through Annie's hands. And then it jerked to a stop.

"Ow," said Annie, looking at her hands.

Then she said, "Dave?"

There was no answer. Annie put the rope down and climbed up onto the chair. She peered into the chute. Her brother was about halfway down.

"I'm stuck," he said.

"It serves you right," said Annie. She got off the chair and disappeared.

The wall was squeezing Dave around his waist. His left arm was jammed down by his thigh. He couldn't pull it free. His right arm was okay, though, and he tried to use it to pull himself up. He kicked his feet. He called his sister.

"Pull on the rope," he called.

Annie's face appeared at the top of the chute.

"Mom's going to kill you," said Annie. Then she threw her end of the rope into the chute and said, "Pull on the rope yourself," and disappeared again. Dave winced as the rope coiled around his shoulders.

He could hear Annie walking down the stairs.

Then everything went deadly quiet.

"What are you doing?" called Dave.

There was no answer. It was black in the chute. Annie had closed the door upstairs, and Dave had dropped his flashlight. He held his hand out in front of his face and wiggled his fingers. He couldn't see them. He couldn't see anything. He was all alone and he was afraid.

Suddenly there were beams of light shooting from below him. Annie had opened the door in the kitchen.

"What are you doing?" said Dave.

"I am making chocolate milk," said Annie.

"You're not allowed," said Dave.

"If you're not nice to me," said Annie, "I am not going to talk to you."

She closed the door and the chute went black again.

"Annie," he called.

She ignored him. She sat in the kitchen and drank her chocolate milk. She left him alone for five minutes.

Now, under most circumstances five minutes is not a long time. But when you are wedged in a laundry chute halfway between where you started and where you were heading and it is black as night and you can't move one of your arms, a lot can go through you mind in a few short minutes.

Like what would happen if there were rats in the chute with you. Or if the house caught fire. Or if your mother never came home. Or worse ... if she did. Dave banged on the wall with his free hand.

"Annie," he called.

No answer.

Five long minutes passed before she appeared at the top again.

When she did, she could hear a strange snuffly sound coming from the chute. She peered down. Her older brother was crying.

"Don't cry, Davy," she said, surprised. "Mom and Dad are coming home soon. They'll get you out."

"But what if they don't?" sniffled Dave. "What if they can't rescue me?"

"They'll save you," said Annie, this time with less certainty. Then she said, "Just wait a minute. I'll be right back."

And her head disappeared from the chute. A few minutes later, the chute door opened again and Annie lowered a little brown lump of something down the chute, attached to a string.

"What is it?" asked Dave.

"It's the ears from my chocolate Easter bunny. I hid them in the bottom of my toy box so you wouldn't eat them."

Dave grabbed the chocolate with his free hand. It was covered with lint and grit. He brushed it off as best he could and took a bite.

"Eat as much of it as you want," said Annie.

After a few minutes, however, Annie could hear her brother sniffling again.

"Dave," she said, "remember when Auntie Brenda sat on the birthday cake?"

"Yeah?" said Dave. He sounded a bit more cheerful.

"And remember," said Annie, "when Mommy dropped the watermelon?"

She went on like that for an hour and twenty minutes.

"Remember when Daddy barfed in the car?"

Annie reminded Dave of all the funny things that she could think of. And when she ran out of stories, she told him every knock-knock joke she knew. Then she launched into the tale of Hansel and Gretel, the way their father told it, where the witch's house was made of Cape Breton shortbread and raisin scones. When she could think of nothing more to say, Annie started to sing. She sang "Jesus Loves Me, This I Know," "Diana" and her favorite, "Splish Splash, I Was Taking a Bath."

When Charlie and Margaret finally walked in the door, Dave was humming along to the theme from the radio show *The Shadow*.

Half an hour later, Charlie was standing in the basement, peering up the chute and poking at his son's small bottom with a broom handle. It was Charlie who guessed that Dave's belt was snagged on some rough piece of the wooden chute. It was Margaret who carefully lowered Dave her pair of sewing scissors and told him how to cut the belt loops of his pants. And it was Charlie, standing at the bottom of the chute, with his arms outstretched, who caught his crying son and held him tight to his chest when it was all over.

Later that night, as Margaret was tucking Dave into bed and kissing him goodnight, he asked his mother about the Springhill miners.

"Do you think they talked to each other when they were trapped down there?" he said quietly.

"Yes, I do," said Margaret.

"Do you think ..." asked Dave, hugging his pillow. "Do you think they sang?"

Margaret brushed the hair back from Dave's face and smiled gently. "Yes, Davy," she said. "I'm *quite* sure they sang."

And now, some forty-odd years later, Margaret was standing in the basement, shining her flashlight up the dark chute and telling Smith Gardner her rescue story.

"What's the matter with me?" she said. "I'm getting all choked up about a laundry chute."

She dropped the flashlight to her side but didn't move.

"Anyway," she said, "that's the whole story."

Smith Gardner didn't say anything. Instead, he reached out and took Margaret's hand. They stood there for several minutes more, looking up at the small bit of leather belt still hanging in the chute. Then Smith moved over to his toolbox.

"Are you sure it's okay that I start?" he said.

Margaret smiled at him and nodded. "You get going," she said. "I'll go upstairs and make tea and fix a snack for when you're finished."

PART V

ARSON, THEFT AND PETTY CRIME

THE PHONE MESSAGE

A tale of desperation that, despite some very fine writing, stretches even the author's credulity and should have, in his opinion, been left out of this volume, as no doubt many will agree. It is presented here at the insistence of the publisher, who believes it might afford a useful lesson to those whose habit it is to speak without thought.

It began simply enough. It began with a phone call—or a phone message, actually. Dave came home and the message light was blinking. So he picked up the phone—the cordless phone (that part is important)—thinking maybe it was Morley.

He was walking around the kitchen with the phone to his ear the way you do when you're a bit keyed up, flipping through the mail, opening the fridge, pacing. He walked into the living room, then over to the kitchen window, not really paying attention to the phone. (That part is important too. That part is maybe the most important part—if, that is, you're interested in the archaeology of the infamous events that unfolded at Dave's house on the night in question. If you're interested in sorting out the spaces between cause and effect, the fact that Dave wasn't paying attention is key, because it wasn't Morley who had left the message Dave was only half listening to—it was Dave's nemesis, his neighbor from two houses down: Mary Turlington.)

It was Friday evening. Mary had called just before she and Bert left town. Her message said, "We are away for the weekend, but we are having a dinner party next Saturday. We'd loooove you to come." Dave was thinking, as he listened to Mary's precise and insistent voice, that he would rather have his legs waxed than go to another dinner party at Mary Turlington's house.

And that's when things began to happen too fast, things that caused Dave to lose his focus. Dave was in the kitchen, sort of listening to Mary Turlington's message, when all hell broke loose. Morley blew through the back door with her arms full of groceries, Sam burst through the front door with two friends, the cat began to howl for her supper …

You don't need all the details. You just need to know that things got confusing for a moment. And Dave, who wasn't paying attention, hung up the phone. Or meant to hang up the phone. The phone, being cordless, requires a person to push a button to hang it up, and, in attempting to hang up, Dave pushed the wrong button. He pressed the call-back button.

So instead of hanging up, Dave called Mary Turlington—or, more to the point, Dave's phone called Mary's message machine. And Dave, who was holding the phone in his hand, waving it in front of himself like a microphone, said to Morley, who was unloading the groceries on the counter, "Mary Turlington has invited us to a dinner paaawty ..."

Dave dragged out the words derisively, as if Mary had invited him over to deworm their dog. He didn't stop there. He kept going. "She says there will be interesting people ... which means there will be name tags. Which means she decides where we sit. And there won't be enough food. There is never enough food. And she never opens the wine anyone brings."

(It's true. She doesn't. The Turlingtons serve Bert's homemade wine—and Bert's homemade wine tastes like car wax.)

And Dave didn't stop there. Dave kept going. Dave said, "I would rather have my nose pierced than go to another party at the Turlingtons'."

And that is when the phone receiver that Dave was waving around beeped. Twice. Dave looked down at the phone, perplexed. That didn't last long. In an instant, realizing what he had just done, Dave was staring at the phone in terror. He had just left Mary Turlington a message.

He had just told Mary exactly what he thought of her dinner invitation.

When the enormity of the moment became clear to him, Dave began to rock back and forth. He stood in the middle of the kitchen, staring at the phone, rocking back and forth. Morley stopped what she was doing with the groceries and watched. When he began to moan softly, she said, "What now?"

"Right," said Dave. "Oh," said Dave, pulling himself together. "Oh," said Dave, straightening his swaying body. "I really don't think I want to go to the Turlingtons' for dinner."

"Get over it," said Morley.

"Right," said Dave. "Get over it. It's nothing. I'll get over it. It's okay."

But it wasn't okay. Dave wasn't about to get over it. And it certainly wasn't nothing. It was something. And Dave knew he was going to have to do something. The potential for gossip was too horrible to consider. If Mary heard the message, if the story got out ... Who was he kidding? Of course the story would get out. Even Morley would be outing him once she heard what he had done. She would be propelled by the universal, indisputable, undeniable drive all women share: the dreaded need to tell other women embarrassing stories about their husbands.

Mary and Bert were away for the weekend. Dave had forty-eight hours to get into the Turlingtons' answering machine. Forty-eight hours to erase his message.

The first thing that came to Dave's mind was that he had to get his hands on the Turlingtons' secret code. If he could intuit their PIN, he could get into their message service and erase his message. He wasted the first half of Saturday morning trying to ferret out the year Mary and Bert were born.

No one seemed to know, although everyone wanted to know why it mattered to Dave. So he gave that up and tried to dial directly into the system, planning to plug in numbers at random—1958, 1959, the Turlington twins' names. Whatever.

But he couldn't find his way in. The Turlingtons didn't seem to *have* a message service. And that's when Dave remembered.

The Turlingtons didn't have an answering *service*—they had an answering *machine*. It was one of those Mary things that made Dave crazy. "It's *waaay* cheaper," she had said dismissively the night Dave spotted the old tape machine in their upstairs family room.

For the first time since Friday night, Dave felt a flicker of hope. He didn't need a secret code—he just needed to get into the Turlingtons' house. If he could get into their house, he could erase his message with a push of a button.

It was Saturday night. Morley wanted to go to a movie. Dave said, "We should stay home. We should rent one." She said, "The one from France." He would have rented her anything. He waited until she was engrossed before he slipped out.

He circled the Turlingtons' house starting in the back-yard, shaking doors, pushing on windows. The Tur-lingtons' house was locked up tighter than a bank.

"Trust Mary," muttered Dave, his hand on the front-door handle, shaking it desperately, until he spotted Polly Anderson watching him from the sidewalk.

"No one's home," said Dave, trying to pull himself together. "All the doors are locked," said Dave.

Then he dropped his voice an octave and said, "I was just checking. Security. Making sure."

Then he said, "Shut up." He had intended to say it silently. He intended it as a personal order, but he was so wound up he barked it out loud.

Polly began to back away.

It was half an hour later, wandering through the park, Arthur the dog by his side, the empty swings hanging glumly in front of him, that Dave had his brainstorm.

He was whistling when he came home.

"What are you whistling?" asked Morley.

"Dixie," said Dave, throwing his jacket across the room, watching it float above the easy chair like a big black bird before it fell onto the arm, perfectly.

"Bingo," said Dave.

Magnetic recording tape, the kind in the Turlingtons' answering machine, is essentially a ribbon of microscopic iron filings. When you record something—say, for instance, an incriminating phone message—the tape recorder organizes the filings on the tape into a recognizable pattern. If you want to erase what you have recorded, you just have to pass the tape over a magnet. The magnet returns the filings back into an unrecognizable pattern.

If Dave could get a magnet, and if he could get the magnet into the Turlingtons', he could erase his message. Heck, if the magnet was powerful enough, he could, hypothetically, erase the message from *outside* the house. Hypothetically.

He tried a building-supply store the next morning. They didn't have the kind of magnets that Dave was imagining.

"This will pick up two hundred pounds," said the guy at the counter.

"Stronger," said Dave.

"Not here," said the guy. "Try a scrapyard. They have magnets strong enough to lift a car."

The scrapyard guy had a greasy ball cap pulled so low over his brow that he had to lift his head to look at Dave. When Dave told him what he wanted, scrapyard guy Steve (at least that was the name stitched on his blue jacket) lifted his head and squinted. Then he walked away without a word. Dave wondered what he was supposed to be doing, until Steve motioned with his head. *Follow me.*

Dave followed him into a dark and dirty back room, a room piled with old engines and car doors and stuff that used to be something but wasn't anything anymore. The guy pointed with his head at a device the size of a wastepaper basket hanging from the ceiling.

"Like this?" he asked.

"Exactly," said Dave. "Could I borrow it for a couple of hours? I'll pay you."

"Seventy-five dollars," said the guy. "And you have to have it back by closing."

"When do you close?" asked Dave.

The guy started to laugh. The laugh became a cough, one of those raspy coughing fits you're afraid is never going to stop. Dave wondered if the guy was going to die right there in front of him, his belly hanging over his belt. Dave thought maybe he should get some water. But then the guy stopped coughing, spat on the floor and said, "We never close." He was shaking his head. Then he reached up and yanked a rusty chain pulley to lower the magnet. "You have to be careful wit' it," he said.

"I can handle it," said Dave.

The guy gave Dave a close look from under the cap.

"I'd better show you," he said.

He lugged the magnet into the shop and set it up on a counter, waist high. He unwound an extension cord and turned around to plug it in. Dave was thinking he should show this guy that he knew what was going on. When the guy turned around, Dave was flicking the switch to turn on the magnet.

And suddenly, Steve, or whatever his name was, who had barely said a word, who hardly moved when he moved—suddenly slow-moving, say-nothing scrapyard Steve exploded.

"NO!" he shouted, jumping back, his arms flying down to protect his waist.

"Huh?" said Dave.

There are many fundamental laws of physics. The magnet knew only one of them. The magnet knew only the law that was in its nature to obey: the law about magnetic fields and the forces of attraction between opposite poles—like, say, an electromagnet and a belt buckle. *Dave's* belt buckle. Dave flicked the magnet on, and slow-moving guy behind the counter threw his arms to his waist and said, "NO!" And then it's hard to say exactly what happened next, except that the magnet flew off the counter.

Dave would later liken it to a wolverine. It flew towards him viciously. There was a whooshing sound as the magnet smacked into him and all the wind left Dave's body at once. His knees buckled, and he sank to the ground, pawing at this thing drilling into his groin like ... like a wolverine.

Dave was dimly aware of slow-moving guy hovering over him, wheezing and coughing and wrestling with the magnet, trying to get at the on/off switch while Dave flailed around in panic.

Later Dave would try to explain it away. "It was a sucker punch," he would say.

In any case, when he got off the floor, regained his wind and brushed himself off, Dave had to convince the guy that he *could* handle it. He eventually talked Steve into letting him take the magnet home, but it was a close call. Seventy-five dollars' rent and a four-hundred-dollar refundable deposit.

"Just bring it back," said the guy, smirking.

Once he got it home, Dave decided he had better try out the magnet before he hauled it up a ladder.

He had jury-rigged a carrier that he was going to use to get the magnet up the ladder to the Turlingtons' den window. It was one of Sam's backpacks, which he was wearing over his chest like a Snugli. He had removed his belt and his watch. He had emptied his pockets of everything. There was zero, none, *no* metal on him at all, not anywhere.

And there was no one home.

He went into his kitchen and he switched the magnet on. There was a high-pitched electric sort of hum, but nothing dramatic happened. Dave smiled. *I can handle this,* he thought. And then he gasped.

Out of the corner of his eye he spotted a carving knife flying across the kitchen toward his chest—blade first. He twisted at the last moment, and the knife flew by him and stuck in the kitchen wall. Now he was facing the stove and a frying pan was making menacing movements. He spun again and cans started sailing out of the recycling bin, hitting him in the chest, attaching themselves onto the magnet and then onto one another. Dave kept twisting. Things kept flying. Dave fumbled for the off switch while lunging around the kitchen, trying to reach his arms around the growing layer of tin cans, slotted spoons and pot and pan lids that festooned his torso. He looked like a piece of modern art, something you might see in an experimental gallery. Metal Man.

It was 6 P.M. before he propped the ladder against the Turlingtons' house. He hitched up his beltless pants and gave the ladder a shake to make sure it was secure. He was pretty sure he had taken care of every variable imaginable. He went over everything one last time. There was absolutely no metal on his person. No belt, no pens, no watch ... nothing. Unlike in the kitchen, there was no metal in the vicinity—nothing loose, anyway. He had borrowed an old wooden ladder from Carl Lowbeer.

He started up, playing out the extension cord behind him. The magnet was protruding in front of his belly like an udder.

He braced himself in position in front of the den window, and then looked around one last time. He took a deep breath. He shut his eyes.

He had already been up here twice without his equipment. He had checked the window frame; it wasn't metal. It was some sort of polyvinyl plastic. There were no overhead wires and no TV antennae. He had thought of everything.

He flicked on the magnet.

He had thought of *almost* everything.

Mercifully, things happened so fast that Dave had no idea what was going on until it was over. He knew only that when he flicked on the magnet, he was ripped off the ladder and flying through the air like a space monkey, as if he had a jetpack on his back. He sailed through the air until he smacked into the side of the Turlingtons' house, where he stuck solid—or the magent did, securing Dave to the Turlingtons' drainpipe.

He was dangling a good fifteen feet above the ground, and arched backwards like some sort of hideous marsupial, all arms and legs and drooling horror, when his beltless pants dropped down around his ankles.

As Dave was hanging from the drainpipe, upside down, wondering what horrible thing he could have possibly done in some previous life to have deserved this, Polly Anderson was making her way down the driveway.

Polly was coming to the Turlingtons' to feed their cats, but Polly wasn't thinking about cats. She was thinking about raccoons. Polly is terrified of raccoons. There are a number of things she hates about them—how their eyes glow unnaturally in the dark, the way their paws look like tiny wizened hands, their pointy snouts. But most of all, what Polly hates about raccoons is their lack of fear. Despite the fact that she is terrified of them, every raccoon she has ever encountered seemed to regard her as a nuisance rather than a threat. As far as Polly Anderson is concerned, an animal so at odds with the natural order of things is not to be trusted. She had spotted a raccoon on the street just the night before, glaring at her as if he'd like to take her on. Tonight Polly was on high alert.

So when she walked directly under Dave, with raccoons on her mind, and Dave's pants finally slipped loose and landed on her back, Polly thought she had been ambushed by the wily street raccoon from the night before. As she lifted off the ground and screamed, lights flicked on all over the neighborhood.

Polly was heading down the drive, batting at the pants that were flapping around her head when she stopped abruptly, untangled herself and looked up.

All Dave could think was, *Of all the days to have put on the white boxers with the red Santa and the prancing reindeer.* And all he could think to say, hanging there upside down in his boxers, was, "Hi."

Then, without thinking, he switched off the magnet.

Jim Scoffield arrived just as Dave hit the ground. Jim pried the Turlingtons' keys out of a shaken Polly's fist and said, "You go home and I'll deal with this." Jim didn't say anything as he helped Dave up and waited for him to regain his wind. Ever since he witnessed Dave in the lobby of the Plaza Hotel with a turkey under his arm, Jim has made it a policy not to ask about Dave's private activities. He didn't comment when Dave followed him into the Turlingtons' house.

"I need a drink," said Dave. Jim didn't notice him slip upstairs into the den.

Dave didn't have time to work out how to erase the messages. Instead he opened the answering machine, thinking he would take the tape home, erase it there and return it later. There were, however, *two* tapes in the machine. One was for the Turlingtons' greeting, the other to record the messages. There was no way to tell them apart. So Dave grabbed both tapes. Before he left, he unlocked a window at the back of the house so he could get back in.

It was after ten when he squirmed through the window with both tapes in his pocket. He was in and out as fast as he could, locking the window he came in through and leaving by the back door. He locked that too. He had one last thing to do.

He hadn't been able to erase his message. There were other messages on the tape, and he had decided he shouldn't ruin them. Instead, he had cued up the message tape to the beginning of *his* message. What he had to do now was go back to his house, phone the Turlingtons and record a new message over it.

He ran home, gathered himself and dialed the Turlingtons' number. The phone rang. Once, twice, three times. He heard the thump and whir of the message machine picking up. Just in time, too.

Out the window, he could see the Turlingtons' car pulling into their driveway. As he watched, Mary Turlington walked up her front steps with her keys in her hand.

The Turlingtons' recorded greeting began. This time, Dave was paying attention, thinking that if he had only paid attention the first time, none of this would have happened. Except it wasn't Mary Turlington's voice he was listening to. It was his own voice. He had answered the Turlingtons' phone, and he was saying, "Mary Turlington has invited us to a dinner paaawty ..."

He was dragging out the words derisively, as if Mary had invited them over to deworm the dog.

Dave had reversed the tapes. He had put the tape with his offending message in the greeting slot. Until someone changed it, everyone who phoned the Turlingtons would be greeted by Dave, and he would be saying, "There will be name tags. She will decide where we sit. There won't be enough food. There is never enough food. She never opens the wine anyone brings."

And he doesn't stop there. He keeps going. He says, "I would rather have my nose pierced than go to another party at the Turlingtons'."

Dave began to rock back and forth. "Oh my God," he moaned. "Oh my God."

A SCIENCE EXPERIMENT

*Including a more faithful account of the arrival of
Sam's friend Murphy than offered in previous
books, and the real truth behind the terrible
events that befell the boys in the basement; a
morality tale of sorts, which will strain the belief
of readers who have never been boys but that,
truth be told, transpired more or less the way
it is presented.*

During French class, Murphy wrote something on a small
piece of paper and folded the paper in half. Then he
folded the paper in half again and wrote Sam's name on
the front. He tapped Ellen Paltiel on the shoulder. Ellen
slipped the note to Robbie. Robbie gave it to Andy. Andy
gave it to Toby. Toby waited until Mrs. Hayes's back was
turned, and then Toby handed it to Sam.

Sam had been watching as the note made its secret
passage across the class. When it finally arrived, Sam
didn't look at it immediately. Instead he slipped the note

onto his lap and leaned forward, staring at Mrs. Hayes. Then, without looking down, his eyes still on his teacher, Sam unfolded the paper. He waited for Mrs. Hayes to turn towards the blackboard before he glanced at it. The page was blank. Sam looked at Murphy and frowned.

Murphy rolled his eyes in exasperation.

Sam looked back at the note in his lap. He turned it over.

There were six words written on the page. *I have to talk to you.* Sam looked at Murphy and nodded. He mouthed a word. Murphy nodded back. The word Sam had mouthed was "Recess."

Sam and Murphy met every recess. This recess, however, they met where they meet when they have *important* business—at the far end of the playground, under the tree where they first met. That was the autumn Sam's best friend, Ben, moved away, the autumn Sam had found himself without a friend in the world.

Until Murphy came along.

Murphy arrived out of the blue, from Winnipeg, and, on his very first day at school, struck out at soccer baseball. After Murphy's second whiff, the gym teacher, Mr. Lovell, who was pitching, rolled the big white soccer ball towards Murphy extra carefully, trying to make it as easy as possible to kick. Murphy, chewing his tongue anxiously, took an awkward hop and kicked at the ball a full second and half before it reached the plate. Then, propelled by the forward motion of his kick, Murphy collapsed in a cloud of dust. It was a feat of athletic ineptitude of staggering proportions.

Later that day, as they ate their sandwiches in the staff room, Mr. Lovell told Murphy's teacher about it. He said he couldn't remember a student *ever* striking out in soccer baseball.

"Never, ever," he said, shaking his head. "If the ball just hits you, you have a good chance of making it to base."

"Did they tease him?" asked Mrs. Estabrooks.

"No one said a word," said Mr. Lovell. "Everyone was too stunned."

Murphy was doomed, however, and the teasing would have begun soon enough. But before it did, word spread around school that Murphy was a special-needs child. And instead of teasing him, kids began looking out for him, *giving* him stuff—candy and little toys—offering him the small kindnesses they might offer a little brother. It was only months later, when Sam and Murphy were best friends, that Murphy told Sam that *he* had started the special-needs rumor himself.

Sam and Murphy met the day after the infamous game of soccer baseball. They were both in desperate need of a friend. When Sam looked up from under his lonely tree and saw Murphy staring at him, he had said, *"What?"* Murphy held up his hand pathetically, nodded at the yard of kids playing tag and shrugged. That was more or less all it took.

Now, a year and half later, Murphy and Sam were friends—best friends—and it was recess again, and they were standing under the very same tree.

Murphy was looking at Sam earnestly.

"I have made an extraordinary discovery," he said.

"What?" said Sam.

"You have to swear to secrecy," said Murphy.

"I won't tell anyone," said Sam.

"You have to swear," said Murphy.

"I won't tell," said Sam.

"Not good enough," said Murphy. And Murphy walked away.

At lunch, Sam said, "Okay, okay. I swear."

"Too late," said Murphy. "You had your chance."

It took Sam two days to wear Murphy down.

"I *promise*," he said, standing in front of him in the hallway. "I won't tell anyone."

Murphy glared at Sam in his owlish way.

"I was in our basement," said Murphy, finally. "I was looking for Christmas presents. I found my father's old chemistry set."

"Why were you looking for Christmas presents in April?" said Sam.

"I sweep the house every spring," said Murphy. "Every year, at Christmas, my parents buy stuff, then they hide it and forget about it."

"Did you find anything?" said Sam.

"I already told you," said Murphy. "I found my father's old chemistry set."

"What about presents?" said Sam. "Did you find any presents?"

"You know," said Murphy, with affection, "you just missed the important part again."

"Sorry," said Sam.

Murphy shook his head. "It's okay," he said. "It's one of the pros of you."

Then Murphy said, "There is stuff in those old chemistry sets they wouldn't let kids near these days."

"Like what?" said Sam.

"You see," said Murphy. "You *can* do it ... when you concentrate. There's carbon powder. There's a sealed bottle of carbon powder."

"Am I supposed to know the significance of that?" asked Sam.

"The significance," said Murphy, "comes when we find powdered sulphur and some potassium nitrate. Once we do that, do you know what we have?"

Sam shook his head.

"We have ... gunpowder," said Murphy.

"This," said Sam, smiling, "is just one more example of why you are my best friend."

They spent an hour and a half in Sam's basement after school. They *didn't* find an old chemistry set. But they did find three Christmas presents stashed in the middle of a box of linen.

"See?" said Murphy.

"I don't believe this," said Sam. "Why didn't anybody tell me about this before?"

They were on Sam's bed, lying on their backs with their feet propped on the wall.

They were eating a stale chocolate Santa.

They were trying to decide on another basement where they might find another old chemistry set—a set that might contain powdered sulphur or potassium nitrate.

"They never put all three ingredients in the same sets," said Murphy. "They spread it around."

"How do you know this stuff?" said Sam.

Murphy pushed up on his shoulders so he was almost doing a headstand.

"It's important," he said. "If someone doesn't hold on to knowledge like this, it will be lost forever."

Then he leaned his back into the wall and fell over slowly so he was kneeling on the bed.

"*Your* dad was a long shot," said Murphy, "but we had to be sure. We're going to check Peter Moore's basement next."

Of all the basements where you might expect to find the missing ingredients for a gunpowder recipe, the Moores' basement is surely the last on earth that would come to anyone's mind. When Peter was born, Mrs. Moore paid a consultant two thousand dollars to "baby-proof" their house. Today, more than a decade later, there are still protective plugs covering all the electrical outlets and plastic bumpers over the corners of the kitchen table. The water heater at the Moores' is set so low, it is impossible to have a decent shower without freezing.

Although the chance of finding anything combustible in Peter Moore's house was slim, Murphy had his reasons for calling on Peter next.

Peter Moore is a slight and nervous boy who was home-schooled until grade five. Even now, you couldn't say he is completely part of the system. Whenever there is a hint of disruption to the school routine, Pete's mother keeps Peter home.

Peter was the only kid in the class who was not allowed on the annual field trip to the caves at Rattlesnake Point. Last year, when everyone else went on a weekend camping trip to the caves, Peter stayed home and read, aloud, from *The Complete Shakespeare Tragedies for Children*.

This of course meant that the following Monday, when everyone at school was still babbling about the camping trip, Peter was left quiet and sad and alone on the sidelines. Which was when Murphy ate lunch with him for the first time.

Peter turned out to be awkward, but kind and smart and funny. And Sam and Murphy started to play with him.

There were, of course, no chemistry sets in Peter Moore's basement. But it was Peter, hanging upside down by his knees from the swing set in the park, who said, "What about Yesterdayville?"

"You're brilliant," said Murphy.

The three boys went home and got their bikes.

They rendezvoused back at the swings a half hour later.

Yesterdayville is a vintage toy store: View-Masters, Lionel trains, a Red Ryder lunchbox, original Chatty Cathys.

And, sure enough, hanging on the wall behind the counter, there was a blue metal box the size of a phone book. The boy in the picture on the front of the box was wearing a bright red sweater vest dotted with a few small rust spots. The boy was holding a test tube.

"Houston," said Murphy, "we have lift-off."

The vintage chemistry set cost seventy-nine dollars.

"We can't afford that," said Peter.

"Don't worry," said Murphy, "we don't have to buy it. Your mother is going to buy it for us."

"No way," said Peter, sounding instantly defeated.

No doubt about it, Jenny Moore is a worrywart. And her son, Peter, suffers for it. Peter isn't the only one who suffers—everyone in Jenny Moore's orbit ends up feeling defeated and inadequate. Sometimes it seems that whenever anything goes wrong in the neighborhood, Jenny Moore is there to offer editorial comment. When little

Fatima Chudary tripped in the park, her mother, Rashida, had hardly had time to chastise herself for not being right by her daughter's side when Jenny Moore appeared, shaking her head. "Well," she had said helpfully, "that's why I never let my Peter out of reach when he was that age."

When one of the Turlington twins got chicken pox the week before Christmas, Jenny Moore nodded knowingly to Mary Turlington. "That's why I *never* let my Peter go into department stores at this time of the year. It's too crowded."

And when Ruth Kelman's daughter swallowed a plastic Barbie shoe, Jenny Moore didn't hesitate to point out that the only toys she ever allowed in *her* house were large wooden handmade things.

"There is no way my mother is buying a chemistry set," said Peter again.

But two weeks later, there was Jenny Moore, walking out the front door of Yesterdayville with the vintage chemistry set tucked under her arm.

Murphy dreamed up the sales pitch, but it was Peter who closed the deal.

"Tell her it's from the 1950s," said Murphy. "Tell her it's *educational*."

"Maybe," said Peter, suddenly hopeful. "Maybe," said Peter again, "that might work."

Peter had recognized the effect the words "chemistry" and "educational" could have on his mother. Indeed, when he brought the subject up the next day, confident, self-satisfied, self-righteous Jenny Moore had been flooded with guilt.

Although she believed with all her heart that no one could teach her child better than she could, Jenny Moore also knew that she had neglected Peter's scientific education when she had home-schooled him. She had neglected it because she herself had, at best, an imperfect grasp of the world of science.

Jenny Moore remembered precisely nothing of science from her own schooldays. She had found every second of biology, chemistry and physics so utterly baffling that the only image she could conjure up of her high school science lab was of an experiment in which she had poured a vial of something into another vial of something, changing the first something from a clear liquid into an extremely pleasant shade of blue. In fact, it was "science," or the lack thereof, that had eventually forced Jenny Moore to abandon her teaching position and send Peter off to the harsh world of institutional education.

So when Peter came home and mentioned that he thought he might be lagging behind the class in science, that all the other kids had been doing simple science experiments for years, Jenny Moore, overcome by guilt and self-doubt, did not pause for a second to consider the dangers lurking in a vintage chemistry set.

And so the three boys gathered, two weeks later, on a Tuesday afternoon after school. They gathered in Peter's basement, and they opened the chemistry set as if they were opening the Arc of the Covenant. On one side there was a Bunsen burner, four glass test tubes, a pair of tongs, a candle and a can of alcohol fuel.

"Jeez," said Peter. "Life *was* better then."

There was also a bottle brush, two instruction manuals and twenty-two miniature brown glass bottles full of exotic chemicals.

One of the bottles was marked *potassium nitrate;* another was marked *sulphur.*

Murphy beamed.

"Stand back," said Murphy.

Murphy took the jar of carbon powder from his pocket and emptied it into one of the test tubes. He added an equal measure of sulphur and tapped in some of the potassium nitrate.

He held the test tube up.

"Voilà," he said proudly.

It was Sam who said, "Now what?"

Murphy, of course, had never considered the "now what." Murphy had been driven by the force of pure science. Holding a test tube full of gunpowder *was* the "now what" as far as Murphy was concerned. The possession of this thing was all the payoff Murphy needed.

It was Peter who said, "What happens if you set it on fire?"

"It would flare up," said Murphy.

"Like what?" said Sam

"Like … a flare," said Murphy.

The three boys looked at each other.

"We need matches," said Sam.

"We don't *have* matches," said Peter. "My mother is opposed to matches."

"What if you want to light candles?" said Sam.

"She's opposed to candles too," said Peter.

"Ahem," said Murphy. Murphy was holding a package of matches.

Peter said, "What if my mother comes downstairs?"

And so they retreated to the safest place they could think of: the furnace room. Peter shut the door behind them. The three of them kneeled down in front of the Moores' hulking gas furnace. Murphy tipped his test tube of precious gunpowder and tapped some of it onto the concrete floor. He leaned over and lit a match.

The match flared and went out. Murphy lit another match. The same thing happened. He lit a third, and it caught. He held the burning match to the pile of powder. Just as Murphy had predicted, the gunpowder flared with a pleasing *whoosh*. The flare was larger than the boys had imagined. It was like the flare from the back of a spaceship. It flared up, and then it went out, leaving the edgy smell of sulphur hanging in the furnace room.

"Again," said Peter, grinning like a boy who had lived all his life in a cave. As if this were the original discovery of fire.

Murphy tipped more powder onto the furnace-room floor and struck another match. Just like the first time, the match fizzled again, but the next one didn't, and Murphy lit the second pile of gunpowder on fire. And then a third.

Murphy held up the test tube.

Murphy said, "There's enough for one more."

Peter said, "Let *me* try."

Murphy gave Peter the matches.

At that very moment, Mrs. Moore was standing at the top of the basement stairs feeling smug. When the boys had arrived at her house, Mrs. Moore had confiscated a large box of Smarties from Sam. Now Mrs. Moore had just finished preparing the boys a snack. She was about to introduce her son's friends to healthy food: she was holding a tray of whole wheat, flaxseed, carob cookies and three steaming mugs of a hot soy beverage.

Downstairs, Murphy was pouring the fourth pile of powder onto the furnace-room floor. Peter had already lit his match. It was burning towards his fingers, and Murphy wasn't going fast enough.

Peter said, "This is the last match."

Peter said, "Hurry up."

Peter could feel the heat of the match on his fingers. He had to do something, or they were going to waste his turn. Peter did the only thing that he could think of doing: he reached out to light the powder that Murphy was still pouring from the test tube.

And that is when Peter's mom opened the furnace-room door.

Murphy was the only one who saw her. He froze. He was holding the test tube at a forty-five-degree angle. The bottom of the test tube was pointing directly at Peter's mom.

In that horrible moment of suspended animation that always signals disaster, Murphy saw what Peter was about to do. Murphy tried to blow out the match.

He was too late.

Peter touched the powder with the flame.

A split second before it caught, Peter's mom looked at the boys crouched on the floor and said, "Snack time."

The powder caught. The little flame burned through the small pile of powder on the floor. The flame burned along the rest of powder, right up into the test tube itself. There was a brilliant flash, and a terrifying clap, and the gunpowder blew out the back of the tube in Murphy's hand.

A bright ball of flame shot across the furnace room—heading directly for Peter's mom.

Mrs. Moore had just enough time to take a step backwards before the ball of fire smacked into the center of her chest.

She grunted when it hit, as if she had been hit in the stomach. By the time Peter and Sam had turned around to look, all that was left of her blue fleece vest was the inside lining and the metal zipper hanging around her neck. The rest of it had vaporized.

Yet *she* wasn't hurt. Not a bit.

Neither was Peter or Murphy. No one was hurt. And no one said a word. Everyone stared for a second, the boys looking directly at Peter's mom, who was still holding the tray of snacks.

Peter's mom was the first to speak.

"Snack time?" she said again, weakly.

And then, as Jenny Moore stood teetering in the doorway, a strange hiss began in the ceiling.

The automatic sprinkler system had kicked into action. Cold water rained down on all of them.

Peter's mom made one last weak noise, more of a squeak than a groan, and she fainted.

The boys looked at Jenny Moore, sprawled amidst the mess of carob cookies and soy beverage.

Murphy said, "Maybe we should go home."

But Murphy and Sam didn't go right home. They helped Mrs. Moore upstairs, her sodden shoes squishing all the way up. While she lay on the couch and Peter stroked his mother's hand, Murphy and Sam cleaned up the spilled snack. As they finished, a fire truck and two police cars screeched up to the house, summoned by the automatic alarm built into the Moores' sprinkler system.

When Murphy finally slipped outside, the street looked like the final scene in an action movie. There were fire engines and two police cars and a group of neighbors who had gathered on the sidewalk. Rashida Chudary was there, and Mary Turlington. Ruth Kelman was just walking over to the house to get a better look. Everyone pressed around wet, bedraggled, pathetic-looking Murphy.

"We didn't know what we were doing," said Murphy, playing to the crowd. "Mrs. Moore bought Peter a chemistry set. She said it was educational. We didn't know that it was dangerous. We were *unsupervised!*"

Jenny Moore phoned Morley that night and apologized in a roundabout sort of way.

"That was satisfying," said Morley when she hung up.

Managing to both execute and survive an explosion in a basement brings a certain amount of notoriety to a boy's life. When Sam and Murphy returned to school on Monday morning, both found their status at school elevated considerably. And Peter ... Well, the science experiment had unexpected benefits for Peter at school *and* at home. When spring arrived that year, Peter was allowed, for the first time ever, on the weekend trip to Rattlesnake Point. And Peter's mom, twitching and fidgeting as she spoke, told Peter he could pack his own lunch for the bus trip. Peter brought just one item: an extra-large pack of Smarties.

CHRISTMAS AT THE TURLINGTONS'

*Containing a faithful account of the catastrophe
at Mary Turlington's Christmas dinner, how
Dave came to be at the Turlingtons' table in
the first place and what possessed him to play
with fire in a way that many readers will find
curious; all written here merely as an
amusement, with no attempt whatsoever
to instruct or improve.*

No one in God's great creation gives themselves over to Christmas more than Morley's neighbor Mary Tur-lington—to the season and the spirit behind it, to be sure, but not only to the season and the spirit: to the whole nine yards, to all the noise that surrounds Christmas.

"I've chosen my Christmas color," Mary announced triumphantly to her husband, Bert, one night last summer.

"I'm doing cinnamon this year."

Notice it's not "we." Not "we are" doing cinnamon. For Mary Turlington, Christmas is a solo sport.

"We'll need a copper tree," she said to Bert a few days later.

And catch that shift: it's an important distinction. Mary writes the score, but Mary expects her husband, Bert, to be in the band. By right of marriage, Bert is enlisted, inducted and suited up.

Mary, who is taken up with and over by Christmas every year, became particularly focused on this Christmas at the end of November.

Until the end of November, Mary believed her mother and her sister and her sister's husband and their four children and her brother and his kids were all coming to her house for Christmas.

But one by one her family had bailed. Her brother got a new job and couldn't afford the time away. Her sister's husband got sick. Her mother said, "I don't know. I don't know. If no one else is coming, maybe I should stay home."

Anyone else might have been disappointed. Anyone else so caught up in Christmas preparations might have fallen apart. *What's the point?* they might have asked. *I work so hard and no one cares.*

Mary didn't fall apart. Mary dug deeper.

"It means we can do things my way for a change," she said to Bert.

Apparently, Mary, who had been all about control, had also been all about compromise.

"I thought I was going to have to do turkey again this year," said Mary. "Emma's so conservative on the question of turkey."

On the question of turkey at Christmas, Bert felt pretty conservative himself. But he was conservative enough not to mention it.

Instead of being unsettled that her plans were unravelling, Mary was becoming unleashed. She was Mary, Unshackled.

"What do you think of henna?" she said to Bert one night.

"Who?" asked Bert.

"If we hennaed your hair," said Mary, "think of how nice you would go with the copper tree."

Mary had, apparently, shifted into some previously undiscovered Christmas gear. And Bert, who had always been delighted by his wife's Christmas cheer, was beginning to feel something that was not delight. It was a bigger feeling than delight, a whirling sort of feeling.

Fear.

Bert was afraid Mary's Christmas was about to overtake him. He felt like the Cadillac in that song about the little Nash Rambler.

"Beep, beep," said Bert.

"What?" said Mary.

"Oh nothing," said Bert.

As Christmas got closer, Mary set out their collection of Christmas candles—a parade of little paraffin men and women in chipped red-and-yellow choir robes.

"I know they are cheesy," she said, "but I love these more than anything."

The candles had been in Mary's family since before she was born. Mary's parents had bought the choirmaster and his wife on their first Christmas together: a man and a women singing their little paraffin hearts out. Mary's mother added to the candle collection each time she had a child.

When her children married, Mary's mother added wax figures for each new husband or wife. And then for each of the grandchildren. After fifty Christmases, there were now twenty-tree candles that lived, eleven months of the year, wrapped in tissue at the bottom of a shoebox, and spent the holiday season marching along the mantel, the two original candles at the head of the paraffin parade.

Only one candle had ever been lit. When Mary's sister's first husband left her for his aerobics instructor, Mary's mother removed his candle from the collection. She burned it in the front window on Halloween. Then she scraped what remained of the candle off the window frame, wrapped the little wax puddle in beautiful gold foil and mailed it to the offending ex-husband the following Christmas.

Ever since then, the candles have assumed iconic status. Every Christmas, Mary's mother picks up her candle and says, "Maybe, when I die, you could light mine and put it on my coffin."

"We'll never light them," said Mary. "Never."

Mary found a local welder to make a copper tree. He came to the house in early December to measure their living room. "I'm going to use steel," he said, "but it will be oxidized steel, so it will be copper-colored. It will look sort of ... sort of ..." He was searching for the right word.

"Dead?" said Bert.

That was the night Mary told Bert she had settled on scallops for Christmas dinner.

"I am going to poach them in saffron," she said, "so they will look nice with the tree."

That was the moment that galvanized Bert. That was the moment he decided the time for action had arrived.

He was standing in his driveway when lightning struck. Not literally lightning, but close. There was a flash and a loud clap, and Bert jumped back, his hands flying up to protect his head. As he stood there, uncertain what had just happened, a giant set of fibreglass reindeer antlers fell out of the sky and planted themselves in the front lawn right beside him.

Bert stared at the vibrating antlers, thinking how ironic it would have been, given his current situation, to have been taken out by a giant Christmas decoration.

Then he looked up and spotted his neighbor Dave running down the sidewalk with his face covered in soot and his eyebrows singed.

"You'll never believe what just happened," said Dave, panting.

It was obvious to Bert what had to be done. Mary needed to be distracted, or Christmas, as Bert knew and loved it, was going to be lost. If Mary's family wasn't going to show up and do the job, Bert needed someone else to take up the slack. Someone to preoccupy her. Someone who rubbed up against his wife a bit, the way her sister did.

"Hey," said Bert. "Dave, good to see you."

And that is why, two weeks later, at two o'clock on Christmas afternoon, Morley looked at her husband across the mess of their living room and said, "If we're going to get to the Turlingtons' on time, we'd better start getting ready."

Dave was standing by the couch in his pajamas, knee-deep in wrapping paper. He was holding his present for Morley. It looked as if it had been wrapped by a small animal with no opposable thumbs.

"This is for you," he said, holding out the package. He kicked his way towards her as if he were walking through a leaf-strewn park on an October afternoon.

"I love you," he said.

Sam, twelve years old and crawling through the paper towards the back of the tree like a caver, stopped dead and looked over his shoulder at his parents. "Will you two please stop talking like that in front of me? It's inappropriate," he said.

At two o'clock in the afternoon at Dave's house, Christmas was still in full swing.

Two doors down the street, however, at the Turlingtons' house, at Christmas central, there was very little evidence that Christmas had ever happened.

The Turlington twins had already taken their presents back to their rooms and put things away in their drawers and cupboards. And while Sam dove under a pile of paper as if he were snorkelling, the Turlington twins, dressed in their matching Christmas sweaters, were at the dining-room table writing thank-you cards. Eighteen-year-old Adam was sitting on the sofa carefully folding wrapping paper and sorting it into two neatly labeled boxes: one marked *recycle* and one marked *reuse*. Mary was vacuuming, in a pair of gold kitten-heel shoes.

And now, these two different cultures were about to be brought under the same roof.

Dave and Morley, Sam and Stephanie, were heading up the Turlingtons' walk.

As they stood on the Turlingtons' stoop, Morley turned and took Dave's arm at the elbow.

"Best behavior," she said.

"Very best," said Dave, nodding earnestly.

He meant it.

They were both thinking of other dinners at the Turlingtons'—of the competitive strain that seemed to hover between Dave and Mary, of the abrasive discussions, political and pedestrian.

Dave took a deep breath.

"Very best," he said again as he reached out and rang the bell.

Mary opened the door. There was an uncomfortable beat before anyone said anything.

Mary was wearing a long black evening gown and gold earrings. Her hair was a strangely artificial shade of orange, sprayed and pulled tightly back into a bun. The expression on her face suggested that she had been expecting the queen but was faced instead with a man from the stables.

If you could have seen inside both of them, Mary in her formal dress and Dave in his cords and a flannel shirt, you could have watched their hearts sinking, both of them thinking, *How did I get myself into this?*

Before either of them had time for a second thought, Dave saw Mary Turlington's Christmas tree for the first time. It had a steel trunk and steel branches and steel needles and steel decorations. Dave, who had been expecting greenery, blinked. To Dave, the tree looked ... rusty. The tree looked sharp, like a kind of giant, corroded medieval weapon. Or a bombed-out electrical tower left rotting in the fields of some war-torn country.

These are the thoughts that were tumbling through Dave's mind as he stood in the hall with his mouth open. And the very first words that came out of his mouth were not "Happy Christmas, Mary," or "Mary, you look wonderful." The first words out of his mouth were "My God ... what happened to your tree?"

Morley saw Mary's jaw twitch. She thought she heard a faraway *whoosh*. It was the sound of an evening of merriment being sucked from the house.

Dave glanced helplessly at Morley.

I'm trying, his expression seemed to say.

Morley stared back: *Try harder.*

Bert ushered everyone into the living room, posing them around the rusting tree, chatting with forced cheeriness. He pulled out his new digital camera. "Everyone smile," said Bert hopefully.

Dave did try harder. In an effort to show Mary that he appreciated her hospitality, he sank his hand into a bowl of gourmet snack mix that was on the hall table. But as soon as he popped the stuff in his mouth he knew he had a problem.

He glanced down at the bowl. There were dried cranberries in there, and what looked like bits of cinnamon stick, but what he had thought were tiny crackers or sweet-potato chips were now looking suspiciously like the stuff you might use at the bottom of a hamster cage. His teeth ground away at what he now realized were cedar shavings. It dawned on him that he was eating Mary's

Christmas potpourri. When he looked up to see if anyone had noticed, he caught Mary staring at him from the living room. Instead of spitting into his hand, which was what he had been about to do, Dave smiled gamely and swallowed.

Bert handed Morley a glass of wine and reached for his camera. "Hold it there, Dave," said Bert.

The more Dave tried, the worse things got.

"Just don't touch anything," whispered Morley, taking a clove-studded orange from Dave's hand.

Everyone was in the kitchen. And everyone was busy. Mary was dusting the turkey with saffron. Morley was tossing the salad. Bert was taking pictures.

"What can I do?" Dave whispered to Morley.

"Just be helpful," said Morley. "Look around for something that needs doing and do it."

Dave couldn't see anything that needed doing in the kitchen. He went into the dining room.

There were flower petals and little pieces of bronze-coloured glitter all over the table.

He went to the hall closet and got the hand vac and hoovered them up.

Then he picked up matches from the buffet and headed towards the mantel. One by one he lit the wicks in the heads of the little wax choir. The twenty-three candles cast a remarkable glow.

A few of the oldest figures burned quickly. The little wax puddles at the tops of their heads sank into their skulls so that the flames of the candles shone through their eyes. It gave them a slightly demonic look. It would be more dramatic, thought Dave, if he dimmed the room lights. Then the candles would be the first thing you saw when you came into the room.

They were certainly the first thing Mary saw when she came through the kitchen doors. She was carrying a salmon appetizer.

They managed to pick most of the salmon up before the Turlingtons' dog got too much. Dave scooped up the biggest piece and wiped it off on a napkin.

"Five-second rule," he said, grinning.

"Hold it there," said Bert, snapping away.

Somehow or other, they managed to get through the meal. After the candles-and-salmon fiasco, Mary had headed back into the kitchen like an army general determined to overcome defeat in the field. Bert kept jumping up at regular intervals and blinding everyone with the flash of his camera. And Morley hung on to her wineglass like a drowning woman clutching a life preserver.

In fact, by the time the turkey was finished, things seemed to have settled down so nicely that Dave felt it might just be safe to help out again. He headed into the kitchen to see about the plum pudding.

"You'll need more than that," Dave offered as he watched Mary sprinkle the pudding with liquor.

Whether or not she needed more is a moot point. The point is, if Mary had just added a little more, everything might have been all right. But she didn't. Mary wasn't about to let Dave tell her how things should be done in her kitchen.

So instead of adding a little more brandy, Mary looked at Dave icily and said, "That will be plenty."

Dave, moved only by the best of intentions, not wanting anything more to go wrong, waited until Mary wasn't looking and gave the pudding an extra shot of brandy anyway. And Mary, not wanting to be proved wrong about how much brandy you needed to light a plum pudding, waited until Dave wasn't looking to give it an extra shot herself.

So the pudding was well and truly soaked when Mary carried it to the table. She did this with great ceremony.

First she called from the kitchen for Bert to dim the lights. She peeked out several times to ask for adjustments. When the lights were just right, Bert got out his camera and positioned himself at the end of the table. When he had finished focusing on where Mary would be standing with the pudding, he called out to her, and Mary, standing tall and regal, like a monarch carrying an orb and scepter, advanced out of the kitchen into the dining room, the pudding proffered in front of her. When she got to the table, she lowered the pudding to the table slowly.

Then she struck a match.

There was a *whoosh* and a flash, and the pudding went up like a Roman candle.

A number of things caught fire.

Perhaps, most spectacularly, and certainly most alarmingly, the cinnamon-coloured silk ribbon that Mary had wrapped around the bun at the top of her head.

The ribbon acted like a wick, and in an instant, blue flames were shooting out of Mary's heavily hairsprayed hair. She stood stock-still by the table, looking like the Statue of Liberty set alight.

Bert was snapping away like a paparazzo.

Unfortunately, it was Dave who put her out.

He used a pitcher of eggnog.

It was hours later, after Mary's hair had been put out and the dining room generally hosed down, the twins in bed and Dave and Morley safe at home, that Mary's sister, Emma, phoned.

Mary took the portable phone into the den while Bert finished tidying the kitchen.

"Emmy sent her love," said Mary when she returned. Her eyes were red. She had been crying.

"I guess I miss her," she said. "I hadn't been missing her at all, but I have never had a Christmas without her. Did you know that?"

"Did you tell her about the candles?" asked Bert.

"And the pudding," said Mary, wiping her eyes on the sleeve of her housecoat. "She reminded me of the

Christmas the dog ate the turkey. And the year Adam knocked the tree over. Remember?"

"Family and friends," said Bert. "They sure mess up our lives."

"They sure do," said Mary. She was smiling now. "They sure do."

THE FAMILY BUSINESS

Wherein Sam is taught—and the reader reminded—that the avails of crime are most certain to disappoint and, moreover, that things are never what they appear to be.

Morley, who hasn't been sick for years, was sitting in a budget meeting at the theatre company where she works, about to get a cold.

Drew, the creative director, was going on and on about the look of next year's brochure. "It's a branding thing," Drew was saying. And Morley, who had skipped breakfast and had only an oatmeal cookie for lunch, wasn't paying attention to Drew. Morley was thinking about a little French patisserie down the street. A place where they make chocolate croissants with a hunk of chocolate stuck in the middle. Drew was droning on about branding, and Morley was so lost in chocolate-longing that she didn't notice the sneeze until it exploded out of her.

It was a sneeze so raw and dramatic, so percussive and impolite, that no one said "Bless you."

Morley was so lost in chocolate that she was as surprised as the others at the table. She looked up and saw that everyone was staring at her.

"'Scuse *me*," she said, putting the emphasis on "me."

Her nose began to run an hour later.

"I'm getting Drew's cold," she said to whomever it was she was talking to at four-thirty.

There is not much of anything you can do to cure a cold. But with the right drugs you can do a lot to hide the symptoms.

Morley stopped at Lawlor's Drugs on the way home.

"This might help," said Doug Lawlor, "and it won't make you drowsy."

"Thanks," said Morley. But as she took the package, Morley was thinking, if she was going to take drugs, she *wanted* the ones that made you drowsy. She wanted something that came with a warning about not operating heavy equipment.

Then she remembered that they needed toothpaste, and then she thought, maybe shampoo too, or was it conditioner? So she got both. She stopped in front of the toothbrushes, and before long, Morley had an armful of stuff.

And that is when her son, Sam, came wheeling around the aisle and almost ran into her.

Sam had come into Lawlor's to buy gum, which he wasn't supposed to have now that he had braces on his teeth. Sam, a pack of Juicy Fruit in his fist, wheeled around the rack of thermometers and spotted his mother just in time.

"Holy," he said, backpedaling around the aisle, out of sight, thinking as he did, *Ditch the Juicy Fruit and bail.*

He was trying to figure out what he should say if his mother spotted *him* when he looked up and spotted *her* himself—in the convex security mirror at the end of the aisle. Except she looked different in the mirror. She didn't look like his mom at all. And in that moment, Sam's heart, which had been saying, *Get going, keep moving,* lost contact with his feet. Sam stopped and stared.

He had never come across his mother like this before— in a public place without her knowing—and he tried to understand why she looked so different. It took only a second for him to realize it wasn't *her*—it was the look on her face, a look he had seen before, but never on his mother. He had seen it on other women, like Mrs. Cassidy, the school principal, and the woman who worked at the sub shop who was always rude to him, and Alexander's mother. Alexander's mother looked like this sometimes.

Sam felt a wave of emotion wash over him. He didn't know what it was at first, just that he was feeling something unusual, overwhelming. Then he recognized it: the feeling was shock.

His mom looked ... unhappy.

He wanted to get out of the drugstore. He wanted to drop the gum and run. But he was mesmerized. He couldn't run.

And that was the moment, while Sam was standing there watching his mother in the security mirror, when Morley, frustrated and tired and beginning to ache all over, her hands full of boxes and bottles, toothpaste and shampoo and a cold medicine strong enough to knock out a trucker—that was the moment when Morley remembered they were out of toilet paper. That was the moment she thought, *I need a shopping cart,* the moment she began to look around to see if there was one at hand.

There wasn't.

Morley was looking for a cart, for anything to unload her armful. But to Sam it looked as if she was checking to see if anyone was watching her. So Sam shrank back against the shelves, keeping his eyes on the mirror.

And what he witnessed next was so outrageous, so beyond the possible, that Sam didn't believe it at first. Right in front of his eyes, his mother, his sweet wonderful mother, took the bottle of shampoo and slipped it into her coat pocket.

Hey, thought Sam, squinting. Then she slipped the toothpaste and the toothbrush and the conditioner and the cold pills into her pocket too.

Hey, thought Sam.

It was like watching one of those video surveillance cameras on a cop show.

It was like the end of the world.

His mother was a thief.

Hey, thought Sam.

And then Morley leaned forward and picked up the pack of toilet paper.

"Not toilet paper," said Sam. He said this out loud. "It's too big. They'll catch you."

Sam wasn't going to stick around for that. Sam wasn't going to be standing by the front door of Lawlor's when the alarm went off and the police came and took his mother away.

Sam turned on his heel and headed for the door.

So Sam never saw his mother empty her pockets at the cash register. He never saw Morley pull out her wallet and pay for everything. Sam was long gone by then.

Sam could barely look at his mother at supper. He ate quickly, his head down, and when he finished, he said, "'Scuse me," and carried his plate to the sink.

When he was halfway there, his father said, "I got a whole box of Chess Records today. First Canadian pressings. Howling Wolf, everyone. I got a Howling Wolf album. Factory sealed."

"Sounds like you got a good deal," said his mother, who seemed jittery. She was fiddling with her hair.

"Good deal?" said his dad. "It was a steal."

Sam dropped his plate.

It smashed on the tiled floor, shards of china ricocheting off the cabinets.

He was living in a den of thieves.

Sam swept up the pieces of broken plate.

"Don't worry," said his mother. She was holding the
dustpan while he chased the last line of dust around the
kitchen. "Don't worry," said his mother cheerily. "There's
more where that came from."

Sam got into bed early, but he didn't get to sleep until
after midnight. He lay under the covers with his eyes
open.

He felt confused. He felt scared. He felt like a moron.

Before bed Sam had slipped into his sister's room. He
had gone through her cupboard. He had gone through her
drawers.

In the drawer of her bedside table alone, he had found
seventeen different types of lip gloss.

No one in their right mind needed seventeen different
lip glosses. Certainly no one would buy that many.

The whole family was in on it.

What had he been thinking all these years? It had been
happening right under his nose, and he hadn't noticed a
thing. He was a fool. His father owned a secondhand
record store ... duh. Where did he think his father got all
those used records?

And the annual yard sale. Where did all that stuff come
from? Sam had never seen half the things his parents
hauled onto the front lawn to sell every spring.

He hit the pillow beside him. *I'm a dope,* he thought.

All these years Sam had thought his mom was just his mom. He had thought he knew her better than anyone in the world. It had never occurred to Sam that his mother did things when he wasn't around. He had thought she worked like his own personal stereo set. He had assumed someone pressed Pause when he wasn't in the room and Play when he came home. He punched the pillow again. He was a moron. He didn't know anything. His mother had more roles in the world than he had ever imagined. One of them, apparently, was master criminal.

Sam lay in the darkness. Maybe he didn't know anything about anything. His head started to spin. He got up to get a drink. It was only when he caught his reflection in the mirror that another thought occurred to him. A darker thought. How come his parents had brought his sister in on the family business and left him out? There must be something wrong with him.

In his heart, he knew what he should do: he should make his mother return what she had taken. He should take her to Lawlor's after school and make her hand over her pile of contraband. She should have to hand it over and say she was sorry and promise she would never do it again.

That would cure her. That's what happened to Sam when Aaron White's mother had found a pack of Ganong chocolates under Aaron's bed, and Aaron had squealed. Sam's father, Dave, had come into Sam's bedroom after he had got off the phone with Mrs. White and said, "You know, I'm really in the mood for a peppermint cream. You don't happen to know where a fellow could get his hands on one at this time of night? Hey?"

Sam hadn't even stolen the peppermints. Aaron White had stolen them, along with the chocolates. But they were hidden in Sam's desk, and Sam had had to get out of bed, go to his desk and produce the box of peppermint creams. Sam's dad made *him* take it back.

But Sam couldn't bear the thought of turning his own mother in. What if they took her to jail?

He told Murphy the next day at recess.

"I saw my mother steal," said Sam.

"I'm not surprised," said Murphy. "I've seen it before. Mothers go through difficult stages from time to time."

"Your mom?" said Sam.

"Yeah," said Murphy.

"Stealing?" said Sam.

"Nah," said Murphy. "My mom did yoga."

"What do you think I should do?" said Sam.

"You could blackmail her," said Murphy. "You could get all sorts of stuff."

At lunch Murphy had another idea. "Crimestoppers," said Murphy. "It's synonymous."

They decided to call from a phone booth—that way the call couldn't be traced.

Sam said, "Someone I know is shoplifting."

"Is this one incident or many?" asked the man.

"I saw *one*," said Sam, "but I think it happens all the time."

"You *saw* one," said the man. "That makes you a material witness."

Sam said, "I want to remain synonymous."

Murphy punched his shoulder. "Ask if there's a reward," said Murphy. "Ask if there's a reward."

"Are you prepared to make a statement?" said the man.

Sam's head was spinning.

"It's my mother," said Sam.

"Your mother," said the man. "Is she a kleptomaniac?"

"No. I think she's from Scarborough," said Sam.

"I mean, is she *always* stealing?"

"Maybe," said Sam. "And my dad. And my sister." It felt good to say it out loud.

"This is different," said the man. "Your mother could end up with a criminal record if the police are involved. That's not nice. But if you don't do anything, she is going to get caught one day."

"What should I do?" whispered Sam.

"This is Crimestoppers," said the man. "This isn't a counselling service. Phone the police and tell them about your mother. Ask *them* what you should do. There are agencies. She probably needs professional help."

By the time he got home from school, Sam felt sick.

There was no way he was going to phone the cops. No way he was going to rat out his mother. If he did that, it would just prove that his parents had been right not to trust him.

It was while his family was eating supper that Sam decided he had to do the right thing. He had to prove he was worthy of being their son.

He would go to Lawlor's.

He would go to Lawlor's *alone*.

He would make them proud.

He would steal something himself.

When dinner was over, Sam put on his coat and his boots and his hat and he headed off into the night. He was terrified. He was excited. He felt alive. And he felt grown up. Very grown up. He would remember this night forever. It was his first crime.

When he got to Lawlor's, he walked up and down the aisles, past the razors and the soaps, past the vitamins, the magazines and the jars of lotions, and he realized there was one major flaw in his plan: he had no plan. He had no idea what he was going to steal. Then he saw the beauty counter, and he knew what he wanted to take. He wanted to take a lipstick for his mother. She would like that. He imagined bringing the lipstick home. He imagined calling his mom and dad to the kitchen. He imagined holding out the tube of lipstick in the palm of his hand. "I stole it," he would say.

They would be so proud of him. They would say they had been dreaming of this day all their lives. They would hug him, and they would tell him everything. They would start taking him on jobs, and he would be really good at it. And one night he would be in the car with his dad, and they would be driving home after hitting a bank or something big, and his dad would say, "We never did anything this big before you. I don't know how we got along without you."

Sam picked up the tube closest to him and took off the cap. It was an electric shade of red, so bright Sam blinked. It reminded him of the light on top of a police car. He put it back quickly. The next tube was a deeper shade of red, a dark reddish brown that reminded him of ... dried blood. He picked up a third tube. And so he was holding two tubes, the dried blood one and one called Forbidden Passion, when he felt his resolve evaporate. Who was he fooling? He couldn't steal. Even if his family were hardened criminals, he wasn't.

Sam went home with nothing.

On the long empty-handed walk home, he tried to figure things out. The whole situation was too complicated to see clearly. He walked the long way and stopped off at the arena. He put a quarter in the candy machine in the lobby and got a handful of M&Ms. He decided if he couldn't do the *best* thing, at least he could prevent the *worst*. The worst thing would be for his mother to get arrested.

When he finally got home, everything seemed so normal. His dad was playing solitaire on the computer, and his mom was lying on the couch with a box of Kleenex. Sam took off his boots and hung his hat on a hook by the door. He went into the kitchen, poured some juice and drank it. Then he went into the living room and crawled up onto the sofa with his mom. She tousled his hair the way she did in the morning before he left for school. Who would do that if she went to jail? Who would wake him up with a kiss? Who would tell him to watch out for traffic?

Sam had to buy his mom some time—at least until he could handle those things by himself.

The next afternoon, Sam came home from school and began to round up the stuff his mother had stolen. He was going to return it to Lawlor's. And he was going to do it without anyone knowing.

But once Sam began to scour the house, everything began to look dubious to him. The new DVD player, for instance. A pair of jeans Dave had brought home on the weekend. The scatter rug in the hall. Arthur's new leash. A bag of salt-and-vinegar potato chips. The toaster.

And then a horrifying thought occurred to him. The very clothes he was wearing could have been acquired through thievery.

Of course, that was the afternoon his father came home early. His father came through the front door and there was Sam, halfway up the stairs, on his way to his bedroom, with the toaster under his arm. He was wearing nothing but his Batman underwear.

Try to explain that.

When Sam had finally deflected all of his father's questions, he retreated to his bedroom. He looked around at all the suspicious things he had gathered from the house. "Give your head a shake," he said to himself.

He had to reduce the loot to a manageable load. He returned everything to its place, except for the six small items he had seen his mother pocket at Lawlor's.

The problem was, everything had been used already. If Sam was going to get this stuff back on the shelves, he was going to have to make everything look new again.

He began with the lip gloss. It was the smallest. It came in a miniature tub with a screw lid. The tub seemed to be more or less full, but the surface bore the telltale sign of his mother's fingerprints. He needed to smooth it off. He touched the top of the lip gloss tentatively with his own finger, but that only made it worse. He tried again, this time wearing a yellow rubber glove he found under the bathroom sink, but the glove made his finger too thick. Then he tried to obliterate the fingerprints by wrapping his finger in Saran Wrap. He only managed to scrape more lip gloss out of the tub. Now it really looked used. The lip gloss was lime green. The only thing he could find that looked even vaguely similar was a tube of Stephanie's hair gel. He squeezed some gel from the tube, filling the tub of lip gloss to the brim and smoothing it off with a knife. It looked overfull, but it didn't look used.

He topped off the shampoo with dish soap, and the conditioner with some of his mother's hand cream.

The tube of toothpaste was easy. He put his lips around the opening and blew into it as if he were blowing up a balloon. It popped right back into shape. He found the cardboard toothpaste box in the bathroom garbage and used Super Glue from his father's workbench to glue it shut.

Next he rinsed the toothbrush off and recovered *its* box and sealed *it* up too. He forgot, however, to dry the brush off, and he did such a good job resealing the container that the toothbrush stayed damp for the three days it hung on the rack at Lawlor's. It was still damp and tasting vaguely of toothpaste when Gerta Lowbeer bought it, brought it home and stuck it in her mouth.

The toothbrush was the first thing that Sam got back onto the racks. Doug Lawlor noticed Sam shortly after that. He thought Sam looked peculiar, moving around the way he was, so Doug kept an eye on him as the young boy hunched in front of the store shelves. With some reluctance, Doug finally asked Sam to show him what he had in his bulging pockets. Sam, of course, had no receipts for what he had, and what could he say? He couldn't tell Doug Lawlor he was *returning* stuff. Sam lined up the toothpaste and the shampoo and the conditioner and the lip gloss on Doug's desk one by one. As he pulled the items from his pockets, he started to cry. Doug didn't know what to do with Sam. He liked the boy. When he asked Sam if he was ever going to steal again and in a very small voice Sam said, "No," Doug got teary-eyed himself. Instead of phoning the police, Doug Lawlor phoned Morley.

"We have a bit of a problem," he said.

When Morley got there, Doug left the two of them alone. Sam told her everything.

"I never ever stole anything," he said. "I was putting it back."

When she finally understood, Morley reached out and pulled Sam to her. "I was wondering what was bothering you."

She told him that she had paid for all of the stuff.

"You just didn't see that," she said.

Sam said, "Oh."

"I have never stolen anything either," said Morley.

"Never?" said Sam.

"Never," said Morley. "But I think a lot of people do. Maybe just once or twice."

"Why?" said Sam.

"I don't know," said Morley. "Maybe because they are feeling sad. Maybe because they think no one loves them, and they deserve to have those things. I think your dad took some stuff when he was a boy. We'll ask him at supper. He'll tell you about his life of crime."

On the way out of the drugstore, Morley stopped to tell Doug Lawlor what had happened.

Sam didn't notice her stop, and he kept walking—past the vitamins and the cold medicines, past the paper towels and toilet paper, where Morley had been standing when he spotted her a few days ago. When Sam realized he was walking alone, he stopped and looked around. He couldn't see his mother anywhere, and he felt a rush of anxiety. But then, just like the first time, he spotted Morley in the big mirror at the end of the aisle. This time, however, she was walking toward him. And this time he felt a wave of relief when he saw her. It was perfect. And part of him wanted to keep her in this view forever— where *he* could see her, and *she* couldn't see him. To have his mother hovering over him the way she was hovering now in this mirror—there, but not quite there—so he could see her whenever he needed to.

Master storyteller and humorist **Stuart McLean** writes and hosts the popular radio show *The Vinyl Cafe*. He is the author of the award-winning and bestselling books *Vinyl Cafe Diaries*; *Home from the Vinyl Cafe*, which won the Stephen Leacock Award for Humour; and *Welcome Home: Travels in Smalltown Canada*. He lives in Toronto, Canada.